Visitor from the Past

Jason started to tremble. Something cold was pressing on the back of his neck. Quickly, he turned to swat whatever it was away. He saw a long wrinkled red trunk attached to a fuzzy round head, a big hairy body crusted with snow and icicles, and a set of four legs, thick as trees. Except for the red fur and the ears that were way too small, it could almost be an elephant.

Eddie rolled over, untangling himself from Jason's legs. "Whoa. T-t-tell me this is a joke, Jason."

How could he? The crazy almost-elephant was tickling Jason's left ear with the tip of its trunk. Now it was pulling on his T-shirt. Jason scooted backward, trying to get away, but whatever it was only took a giant step forward.

"It's not a joke."

"Th-th-then what is it?"

Jason rubbed his eyes. When he finished, the creature was still there. "It looks like one of those mastodons you see in a museum."

"But what's it doing here?"

Jason wished he had an answer.

There's a Mastodon in My Living Room

Elaine Moore

Troll

Due to limitations of space, permissions and acknowledgments continue on page 6.

Dedicated to:

Joyce, there in the beginning and throughout.
Ellen, for plowing through the middle.
Joanna, my saving grace with abundant thanks.
Bob, for his enthusiasm in all things satellite.

But mostly to Elvis Presley with the hope that
my readers will come to know, love, and appreciate
the talent behind his beautiful voice.

Contents

Chapter 1

Jason

You ain't nothin' but a hound dog—
cryin' all the time.

"Jason!" *Twang. Twang.* "The doorbell!"

Jason had heard it. Just like he'd heard every stupid Elvis tape his stupid sister had been playing all stupid afternoon.

Here it was Monday, the first stupid day of stupid summer vacation. The day wasn't even halfway over and already Jason knew this was going to be the stupidest summer of his whole stupid life.

"Jason!" Brandy screamed again from her bedroom upstairs. "The doorbell!"

Jason drummed his fingers on his chest. Why didn't Brandy get the door? So what if he was downstairs and closer. If Brandy was talking on the phone, that wasn't an excuse either, since Brandy was always on the phone. Either that, or the telephone grew out of her ear.

Brandy's new boyfriend, a burger flipper at McDonald's, had only called nine million times in the last half hour. Add that to the five million calls from her other friends since their parents had left for work that morning, and anyone could figure out why Jason never got any phone calls. The line was always busy.

Jason got up. Any other summer, his mother would have answered the door, but she had recently returned to work in a lawyer's office. She said Jason and Brandy were old enough to look after themselves.

"Jason!"

"I got it!"

Jason opened the door. His best friend, Eddie, shuffled through the foyer and flopped on the couch in the living room. Eddie grabbed the remote control and pointed it at the television.

"Hey," Jason snapped. "You know what my dad said. I'm not supposed to watch TV. I'm supposed to be reading."

Jason planned to stay in this rotten mood the whole stupid summer. It was all his father's fault.

Last night, Jason had been sitting cross-legged on his bed watching TV when his father came in. Jason glanced up. His dad was holding out a book.

"Son, we've had this talk before. Your mom and I

are more than a little upset about your final report card. We've worked hard with your teachers and we've tried to be patient, but these miserable grades of yours have gone on too long. Now, I went to the library for you and selected this title myself." His father held the book out, waiting for Jason to take it.

On the TV, just past his father's shoulder, a man in a white coat was hooking a defenseless little monkey to a bunch of wires. The monkey was waving his arms and shrieking. The man walked away, leaving the monkey huddled on a laboratory table.

Suddenly the screen went blank.

"And no television until you're finished." His father reached behind the TV and pulled the plug out of the socket.

"Hey! What gives?"

Then Jason's father picked up the TV and carried it out of the room. Jason couldn't remember the last time he'd seen the top of his dresser. He'd always had a TV there.

"Son, I want you to know, this is not a punishment," his father said when he returned empty-handed.

Jason could barely breathe. What kind of a joke was this? His father was taking his TV and it was not a punishment?

"We don't want you in elementary school for the rest of your life. In another year you should be moving on to junior high, then high school, then college. Your mother and I have been concerned for some time now.

You've had all the tests and there's nothing wrong. It's not that you can't read. It's that you choose not to."

He shook his head. "You're the one who made the deal, remember? Instead of going to summer school—"

"I know," Jason interrupted. "Two books a week for the whole summer."

"Starting when?" Mr. Richards held up a finger. "You don't have to answer that. I'm answering it for you. The book I gave you comes highly recommended."

"By who? Brandy?" Jason held the book up by the tips of his fingers, as if it was contaminated. "*Julie and the Wolves*. That's a girl's book."

"Funny. It wasn't when I was a kid. In fact, I kind of liked it."

"I don't like *old* books either."

"Jase. Let's be honest here. Right now you don't like *any* books. You haven't read a book in so long, you've forgotten how."

"Dad—"

"No. Listen to me. You have to read. You've frittered away your whole fourth grade. This summer is a good time to get back into the swing of things. When you finish this book, you can ride your bike to the library. Twenty-four books this summer. No television until you've read them all."

"So when are you going to be finished?" Eddie said. "Sometime next year?" Eddie set the remote on the coffee table.

Jason glanced at the remote, ignoring Eddie's remark. Any other time Eddie could have roused Jason out of his rotten mood. But no TV for the entire summer was serious stuff. Besides, so what if he didn't like reading? When it came to math, he was a regular whiz.

Unable to resist it any longer, Jason picked up the remote.

"Don't get your hopes up," he told Eddie. "We're not going to watch a whole program. All I want to do is see what we're missing."

Zappo. Zappo, Jason said to himself. He pressed the memory button, switching channels.

"Just as I thought," he told Eddie under his breath. "There's nothing on but soaps."

He was about to put the remote down for good when the TV flickered, then shut off completely. Puzzled, Jason shook the remote and hit the memory button again. Upstairs, the singing and twanging of King Elvis fell suddenly silent.

"Hey, Jason!" Brandy shouted. "What happened?"

"How should I know?" he yelled back. "The electricity went off."

The TV flickered and came back on. *Twang. Twang.* Elvis was at it again. "Never mind, Jason."

"Hey," Eddie sat up, suddenly curious. "Gimme that thing."

Laughing, Jason pulled his arm back, out of reach. When Eddie lunged, Jason whirled. He pointed the remote at Eddie and pressed the button.

13

Zappo! Zappo!

Jason felt Eddie's arms wrap around his ankles. As he went down, he aimed the remote at the TV.

ZAPPO!

"Hey, you guys!" screamed Brandy, louder than ever. "What's going on down there? Quit banging around."

Eddie and Jason were on the floor. Eddie had almost wrestled the remote free when a stiff Arctic breeze whipped through the living room, sending icy shivers across Jason's skin. Magazines and newspapers flew up in small circles, then smacked against the wall in torn, sloppy heaps. The room filled with a strange musky, moldy smell.

Looking over Jason's shoulder, Eddie suddenly stiffened.

Jason started to tremble. Something cold was pressing on the back of his neck. Quickly, he turned to swat whatever it was away. He saw a long wrinkled red trunk attached to a fuzzy round head, a big hairy body crusted with snow and icicles, and a set of four legs, thick as trees. Except for the red fur and the ears that were way too small, it could almost be an elephant.

"Geez . . . Eddie?"

Eddie rolled over, untangling himself from Jason's legs. "Whoa. T-t-tell me this is a joke, Jason."

How could he? The crazy almost-elephant was tickling Jason's left ear with the tip of its trunk. Now it was pulling on his T-shirt. Jason scooted backward, trying to get away, but whatever it was only took a giant step forward.

"It's not a joke."

"Th-th-then what is it?"

"How am I supposed to know?"

"Because it's your house, that's how," Eddie shouted, crawling as fast as he could in the other direction.

Jason rubbed his eyes. When he finished, the creature was still there. "It looks like one of those mastodons you see in a museum, only minus the tusks and a lot smaller."

"You think it's a baby?" Eddie whispered.

Jason shrugged. "Maybe."

"But what's it doing here?"

Jason wished he had an answer.

The fuzzy visitor bobbed its head up and down. Then, before Jason could stop it, the peculiar elephantlike creature stretched its trunk toward the ceiling—and trumpeted.

Oh no! Jason covered his ears. Now what?

"Hey, Jason!" Brandy yelled. "Put a lid on it. You're drowning out Elvis."

Just then, the phone rang. Jason didn't move to answer it. He had other things on his mind. The call was probably for Brandy anyway.

Okay, so maybe the creature really *was* a mastodon. And maybe it wasn't all *that* gigantic, but it was the size of a Shetland pony. It was fat and fuzzy and rust-colored, *and* it was right there in the living room. If his mother found out, she'd have a heart attack.

Eddie's voice started to squeak. "Jase, nothing like this has ever happened to us before. It's almost like it came *through* your TV set."

Jason stared down at the remote, still in his hand. "Shoot!" he said, holding it out toward Eddie. "All I did was switch channels. Hey, what's the matter?" Jason asked as the baby mastodon started backing up, obviously scared.

Quickly, Jason shoved the gadget in a nearby drawer. He didn't want to scare the poor thing.

"Jason," Brandy was chirping like a bird. "Mom's on the phone. She wants to know what you're doing, and I'm supposed to be sure it's only Eddie who's here and not any of your other lame-brained friends. Don't make me come down and check. It *is* Eddie, right? And another thing, Mom says you're supposed to be reading. There's no way you can be reading and making all that noise."

"Yeah, it's only Eddie. Tell her I'm working on a science project," Jason shouted, eyeing the mastodon, who was taking shy steps toward where the boys were sitting.

Suddenly the mastodon stopped. He bowed his red head, looked at Jason with sad eyes, and sniffed loudly.

"Aw, it's crying," Jason whispered. "It's OK, fella. Don't cry. Please don't cry."

When the mastodon hiccupped, Jason felt sorrier than ever. Eddie was right. It was just a baby. Probably it was as scared of them as they were of it.

Jason leaned forward. Slowly he reached out one hand and waited, quiet as a statue, while the mastodon rocked from side to side, whining softly. Then, just when Jason thought he might as well give up, the creature extended his trunk. He took one last step and touched Jason's palm with a tiny flap of skin that curled like a finger from the end of his red trunk.

"What do you know? It's friendly!" Eddie breathed a sigh of relief.

Just then the lights blinked once, twice, three times. Then they went off, and so did Brandy's stereo.

"Jason!"

Great! He could hear Brandy storming out of her room, heading for the stairs.

"Quick!" Jason grabbed the fuzzy little fellow by its back legs and tried pushing it at Eddie. "We've got to get him out of here!"

"Where?" Eddie had a hammerlock around the animal's head. But the mastodon kept swinging around playfully to face Jason.

"Jason! Answer me!" Brandy screamed as she landed at the bottom of the steps.

"I don't know. Anywhere. Out the back door. Hide him in the woods. But be careful," Jason cautioned as the three of them struggled through the dining room. "Don't hurt him. Here." Jason pulled the tablecloth

17

off the dining room table. "Cover him up, in case someone sees."

The kitchen door had barely closed behind the mastodon when Jason found himself staring straight into Brandy's piercing blue eyes.

There wasn't time to brush the red hairs off his T-shirt. He hoped Brandy wouldn't notice.

"OK," she said, hands on hips. "Where is Eddie? Did he leave? What were you guys up to? And don't say 'nothing.' That science project of yours is causing all this trouble. Don't say it's not."

Oh! Jason got it. Brandy was holding him responsible for the problems with the electricity.

"You better quit it," she continued, "before you really mess things up."

Jason wasn't sure how things could get much worse than finding a baby mastodon in the living room. He tried his best to look sorry.

"I'm going upstairs," she said. "If everything's back to normal—including the electricity—I'll forget about calling Mom. And clean up that mess in the living room *now*." Brandy wrinkled her nose disdainfully. "What's that disgusting smell? Honestly, Jason."

It was the craziest thing. No sooner had Brandy left, than the power went back on. It was enough to give Jason the creeps.

Chapter 2

How Do You Care for a Mastodon?

Jason pulled a Snickers bar out of his shirt pocket. He cut the candy bar in two pieces with his pocket knife and handed Eddie half.

"OK, now what are we going to do?" Eddie asked, licking chocolate off his fingers.

The boys were hidden in a clearing in the woods behind Jason's house. The baby mastodon, which they had decided to call Tiny, was sniffing an oleander bush a few feet away. The boys had grabbed some clothesline rope from the utility room and tied one end to Tiny's leg. They took turns holding the other end.

"I can tell you what we're *not* going to do," Jason said, remembering the little brown monkeys in the laboratory cages he'd seen on television the night before. "We're not going to tell anybody. Mastodons are supposed to be extinct. If the wrong people got hold of Tiny, they'd turn him into a scientific experiment. They'd hook him up to wires and machines. Maybe they'd run him on a treadmill. When they were finished, they'd stuff Tiny and put him in the Smithsonian. They'd write his name in Latin on a brass plaque, and I guarantee you the name they use won't be Tiny. Maybe we should just keep him and not tell anybody."

"That's nuts," Eddie said, rolling his eyes. "What about when our parents want us home for dinner and stuff?"

Jason thought a minute. "Today's Monday. Doesn't your mom do something on Mondays?"

"The Million Dollar Club."

The Million Dollar Club was a fancy name for a dumb realtors' meeting. Listening to Eddie, you'd think his mother sold mansions to movie stars instead of houses to ordinary people.

Jason nodded. "Right. And your dad bowls."

"Yeah, he says they're going to win that big . . ." Eddie's voice trailed off. "Oh, I get it. I tell them I'm eating with you, only I mastodon-sit instead."

"Tomorrow it's my turn," Jason said, ignoring Eddie's lack of enthusiasm. Give Eddie a little time and he'd come around like he always did. Having a mastodon for a pet was going to be neat. "The only time our folks check up on us is when we spend the night."

"Glad you brought that up, Jase. If you think my

folks are going to let me spend the summer sleeping in the woods, you're wrong. Even if it is the woods behind your house, they'll never go for it. Your parents won't either."

Jason sighed. "We could tie him to a tree. Nobody comes back here except us. We'd just have to stick around until Tiny falls asleep. You'll see. It'll work out."

But even as he said it, Jason wasn't quite sure. Tiny had finished exploring the trees and bushes and was playing with the empty Snickers wrapper. Finally Tiny picked up the wrapper and offered it to Jason. He sniffed the peanut and chocolate smell still on Jason's hands and nodded his head.

Jason glanced helplessly from his hands to the curious green eyes of the baby mastodon. Tiny was trying to tell him something. Did he want something to eat?

It occurred to Jason that he couldn't go to the store and buy mastodon dinners in a bag the way he might for a dog or cat. Even if he could, except for the five dollars and forty-six cents he kept in his sock drawer, he didn't have any money. There had to be someone he could ask.

"Maybe we should call the zoo," he told Eddie.

"The zoo?" Eddie laughed so hard, he had to hold his stomach. "How many times have you seen a mastodon at the zoo?"

"None." Jason frowned. "But you'd think they'd know."

"Sure, Jase. Why don't you try something simple like the encyclopedia?" Eddie said. "Check it out. You're supposed to be reading this summer, aren't you?"

"Don't preach," Jason said, reminded of the book his father had brought home from the library. "Anyway, whose side are you on?"

Eddie put his hand on his chest and did his best to look innocent. "Yours, of course. No offense, Jase, you might not find anything, but the encyclopedia would be a good place to start."

Jason stood up and dusted off his pants. "OK, you win."

He handed Eddie the clothesline.

Tiny began wailing and thrashing about. *Tramp, tramp, trample, trample.* He rushed over to Jason and wrapped his trunk around him.

"It's OK, fella. I'm coming right back." Jason struggled to wriggle free. Tiny was whining and crying as he looked anxiously from Jason to Eddie and back again. It made Jason feel helpless. What was he supposed to do? He didn't know how to take care of a mastodon.

Jason cleared his throat. "I get it. You want us both here."

Together, Jason and Eddie hugged the furry little fellow. They scratched behind his ears and down his back in an effort to calm him.

"He must be scared to death. Look how he's trembling," Jason said. "Poor little guy. He doesn't know where he is or anything. I bet he misses his mother."

"Maybe he thinks you're his mother," Eddie said. "Give him something that has your smell."

Quickly, Jason took off his T-shirt. He balled it up in his hand and rubbed it along his arms and chest. It should smell as much like him as possible. Then he offered it to Tiny. Magic! With the deepest, most contented sigh Jason could possibly imagine, the mastodon calf snuggled into a bed of leaves, closed his sad-looking eyes, and drifted off to sleep.

A few minutes later, Jason slipped out of the clearing and headed toward home. Somehow, somewhere, he had to find out: How do you care for a mastodon?

Chapter 3

Say It Ain't Hay

I'm a little mixed up, but I'm feeling fine . . .
I'm all shook up.

Jason slipped into the house. He grabbed a clean shirt out of the laundry basket. Brandy was upstairs listening to Elvis and yakking on the phone as usual. Every once in a while he'd hear a shriek followed by a series of giggles. That meant she was talking to one of her silly girlfriends. Brandy didn't shriek when she talked to guys. She only giggled. That was bad enough. Someone ought to do her a favor and tell her she sounded like a hyena.

Still, Jason would have to be careful. He didn't want her to ask any snoopy questions.

Slowly Jason inched his way across the floor toward the bookcase in the upstairs hallway. A TO ANJOU.

ANKARA TO AZUSA. EGYPT TO FALSETTO. There! Volume eighteen. M TO MEXICO CITY. Jason slid the heavy book out onto the rug. Quickly, he flipped through the pages until finally he found a black-and-white drawing of what could easily be Tiny's mother. Jason smiled at his good fortune. But his smile quickly turned into a frown.

The people who wrote the encyclopedia didn't know any more about mastodons than he did. Worse, there was nothing to tell Jason what mastodons liked to eat.

Jason thought about telling his dad that he'd wasted his money. A whole set of books and nothing to tell you how to take care of a mastodon. What good was the encyclopedia anyway?

More Elvis music came from Brandy's room.

> *Where do you come from?*
> *Tell me who you are.*
> *Do you come from another world*
> *or from some distant star?*

Twang. Twang. Blip. Blip. Blip.
"Hold on. I have to change my tape."

Brandy's bed made a spring-sprongy noise as she got up and walked toward her stereo. Jason didn't breathe again until she was yakking away again about a party at DeeDee Morgan's house.

Jason jammed volume eighteen back where it

belonged with the rest of the set on the shelf and inched his way downstairs to wait for Brandy to get off the phone. A party tonight meant . . . yep, the shower was going full blast.

Jason reached for the phone and called the zoo.

"A mastodon? Young man, is this some kind of a joke?"

"No, sir." Jason hadn't told him about having a mastodon. Jason just said, "What if?"

"Just say I had this baby mastodon and I had to take care of it. What would I do? Would I have to take it to the vet to get a rabies shot or something? I mean, what would happen if the mastodon got rabies or something like that? Could it die?"

The man was laughing. "A rabies shot for a mastodon. That's a good one. Look kid, I don't know what they tell you at school, but at the zoo, we're busy. We've got lions and tigers and elephants but no mastodons."

"You've got elephants?" Why hadn't he thought of that before? "Maybe you could tell me how you take care of an elephant. It's for a science project."

A heavy feeling settled in Jason's chest. Normally, he would never lie to a grown-up, but these were unusual circumstances.

Uh-oh. Jason heard the shower cut off upstairs.

"A science project." Jason gulped. "And time's *really* running out."

"Well, then I better get right to it."

Jason took a pencil and paper out of the top desk drawer. As fast as the man talked, he wrote. What luck! If his baby mastodon was anything like an elephant, he had it made. At least that's what Jason thought, until the man got to the part about the hay.

"A grown elephant eats, oh, anywhere from one hundred to one hundred fifty pounds of hay a day."

"You mean a month," Jason interrupted.

"No. A day. You want a month? Let's see, that one hundred fifty pounds would make roughly half a ton a week. Assuming you've got four weeks in a month, that'd be somewhere near two tons."

"Half a—" Jason barely squeaked.

"Ton. You got it. That'd be one week but, like I say, that would be two big ones a month."

"Tons."

"You got it."

"B-but where am I, I mean, where . . ."

"We do go through a lot of hay." The man chuckled.

Jason didn't. Two tons was no laughing matter. He couldn't even think that big. He'd never find two tons of hay. Tiny would starve!

As soon as the man hung up, Jason hurried outside to tell Eddie.

"Two tons?" Eddie yelped. "You've got to be kidding. In a million years, you couldn't find that much hay!"

"Wait a second. He was talking about a grown elephant. Tiny's a baby."

"Yeah, but remember what we saw when we took that field trip to the Smithsonian? Mastodons grow up to be bigger than elephants. Lots bigger! You know what that means, Jase?"

Jason was almost afraid to ask.

"It means Tiny is going to grow and grow and grow. He's going to do it really fast, probably right before our eyes. Boom!"

"No way." But even as Jason said it, he was watching Tiny munching away at the mountain laurel. In a couple of days, there wouldn't be any woods left. Somehow he had to find a way to feed his hungry pet.

Chapter 4

Jason's Promise

Jason was still trying to come up with an answer Monday night as he sat down for supper. His mother was talking.

"The traffic was terribly backed up coming home. I never dreamed the commute would be so awful. I spend all my time sitting in the car," she complained. "I thought widening Maple Avenue was supposed to eliminate the traffic jams."

That was the problem with grown-ups, Jason thought. They never said anything interesting.

His father nodded. "The road isn't even finished, and already they're building another office building on the other side of Maple."

Except for being able to sleep in his jeans, being an adult wasn't much to look forward to.

"That's too close! What ever happened to our

quiet neighborhood?" Mom stopped. "Listen to me. I sound like Marge Huddleston."

Jason's ears perked up. His parents were talking about Eddie's mother now.

"Marge claims Mr. Gammel is destroying our property values with his satellite dish. As a realtor, I guess she should know. The hearing is set for next Friday."

"None too soon either," Dad said. "Looking at that silver dish sitting in his front yard gives me a headache. If we don't stop him, we'll have a line of fifty-foot TV antennas up and down the street."

"Sweetheart, the Homeowners' Association has rules about such things. Remember the covenants we signed? Anyway, Marge called an emergency meeting for Wednesday night. They won't have any trouble making Mr. Gammel take the dish down."

"Good," Brandy said, chiming in. "That thing is so ugly. Whenever DeeDee walks by Gamma Rays's house—"

"Sweetie, his name is Mr. Gammel."

"I know, Mom, but ever since Billy Newsome saw Mr. Gammel with his laser gun, all the kids call him Gamma Rays."

"That was not a laser gun. It was a little flashlight thing that Mr. Gammel invented to use when he took photographs for *National Geographic*. There was an article about it in the *Gazette*. The man is a genius."

"OK, OK." Brandy crinkled her nose in the way that drove Jason nuts. Jason had seen her practice in front of the mirror for hours. She thought it was cute. She was wrong. When Brandy crinkled, she looked like a skinny blond squirrel.

"DeeDee says the satellite dish is like a gigantic eye that follows you down the street. Gamma—er, Mr. Gammel—sits inside his house and spies on us. DeeDee knows because—"

Suddenly, it was like a lightbulb lit up in Brandy's dim brain.

"Wow!" she shrieked. "I bet *he's* the reason the electricity keeps going out."

Dad frowned. "The electricity went out? When?"

Mom was next. "For how long? Did you check the refrigerator? I had ice cream in the freezer."

"It wasn't that long. At first I thought it was Jason because he had the TV on, but we've had both the stereo and the TV on plenty of times."

"Jason was watching TV?" Everything stopped as Dad spoke up. "Son, you were supposed to be reading."

Jason put down his fork. What was the matter with Brandy? The creep. Why didn't she keep quiet and eat her dinner so he could get back in the woods with Eddie? Didn't she have a party to go to? Maybe he should remind her.

"I wasn't watching TV," Jason mumbled.

"Right," Brandy chirped, a satisfied grin on her face. "You're the only person in the world who *listens* to 'General Hospital' for background music."

Jason sighed in defeat. If he had known he was going to have Brandy for a sister, he would have refused to be born. He would have sat inside his mother, arms folded, a determined look on his baby face, and refused to come out.

"Anyway, the electricity went off," Jason said by way of defense.

It worked for the moment. His mother turned to his dad. "You did pay the bill, didn't you? Maybe you should check the wiring. If anything happened to the children while I was at work . . ."

"It's probably nothing to worry about," Dad answered, "but I'll check it anyway. My guess is the disturbance was caused by the construction." He raised his eyebrows at Jason to tell him they would finish their discussion later.

Jason gave Brandy his if-looks-could-kill glare. Of all the people in the world, he, Jason Richards, did not deserve to have a sister. Just because Brandy got straight A's, did that give her the right to ruin his life? Besides, the deal he'd made with Dad was for two books a week. This was only Monday. What was the rush?

Jason glanced out the window anxiously. The sun was starting to set. Eddie would be getting hungry. So would Tiny. Jason stood up. If he moved fast enough . . .

"Son?" Mr. Richards gave Jason a questioning look. "What about the reading?"

"Uh," Jason stammered. "Tomorrow, Dad," he called over his shoulder. "I promise."

"Jason," his father called after him, "I know what you're thinking. You're thinking that all you promised was to read two books each week and this is only Monday. But the point is, you haven't even started and your procrastination has got to stop. Now, if you'll excuse me, I think I'll go downstairs and check the fuse box. After that, I've got some lawn to cut before it gets dark. I'm surprised the neighbors aren't picketing *us*, the way I've let the grass grow as high as hay."

Hay?

Jason stopped in the doorway between the dining room and the kitchen. Had he heard right? Jason felt a wide grin spreading across his face and covered it quickly with his hand. He'd noticed a long time ago, there was nothing that aroused his father's suspicions more than a silly grin.

"I tell you what, Dad," he said, puffing up his chest just enough to remind his father that he was no longer a baby. "Why don't you check the fuse box for Mom like you said. And when you're finished, why don't you just lay your tired body down in front of the television set. Let *me* take care of the yard. I know how. After I mow the lawn, I'll take the grass clippings and put them in the woods. Don't be thinking it's too much work for your son, even if he is only ten years old, because I'm going to get Eddie to help me."

Mr. Richards looked at Jason with a dazed expression.

If Jason had known how much cutting the grass

meant to his father, he would have done it a long time ago. It made him wonder what else he could do to please his dad.

Jason felt so guilty for not telling his parents the *real* reason he was going to cut the grass, he said what he never would have said otherwise.

"Tomorrow, just to make you and Mom happy, I'm going to finish reading that book you selected for me and then I'm going to the library . . ."

Jason stopped. His mom and dad were both staring at him, looking completely dumbfounded, and something else Jason had seen only on rare occasions. They looked *proud*.

"And when I'm at the library," Jason went on, caught up in the grand and glorious moment. "I'm going to . . ."

"Yes, darling. What is it?"

Jason almost choked on the words, but he blurted them out anyway.

"I'm going to check out a book."

Chapter 5

Too Much Stuff

Exhausted from two hours of mowing and raking up grass for Tiny's dinner, Jason let his knapsack drop to the ground. Eddie was leaning against a tree. He was holding a flashlight, and around his neck hung a pair of binoculars. Eddie loosened Tiny's clothesline from around his ankle and tied it to Jason's. It was Jason's turn to be connected to the mastodon.

"So did you bring *me* anything to eat?"

Jason handed Eddie his usual triple-decker peanut-butter-and-jelly sandwich and the canteen filled with grape Kool-Aid. Then he staggered over to Tiny, who had been pulling the leaves off a nearby oak tree.

When Tiny butted him playfully in the chest, Jason laughed. He stepped back to pet the wrinkled space between Tiny's eyes.

"Remember what my dad said when I asked for a

37

puppy last Christmas?" Jason peeked over Tiny's shoulder to catch Eddie's reaction. "He said having a dog is a big responsibility, and since he didn't think I'd ever remember to feed it or take it for walks, it wasn't such a hot idea. If my dad wouldn't let me have a dog, what's the chance he'd okay keeping a mastodon?"

Jason gave Tiny a scratch under the chin before sitting on a log. "When I'm grown up, I'm going to remember what it was like to be a kid."

"Bet you don't." Eddie sat down beside Jason as Tiny turned slowly and began pulling the tender shoots off a young mountain laurel.

Jason watched for a minute. "Bet I do," he said.

"Bet you don't." Eddie picked up a stick and broke it. "Nobody ever does. Not teachers. Not parents. Nobody remembers being a kid except a kid."

Sometimes, for Jason, silence was a comfortable thing. It was that way now as he and Eddie sat on the log and watched Tiny. If they'd tried, they couldn't have kept their eyes off him. Everything Tiny did—the curious tilt of his head, the playful flick of his tail—everything was a small miracle.

Eddie checked to be sure Tiny had enough water in the trash can they were using as a water bowl. Then Jason slipped the clothesline leash off his ankle and tied it around a good strong tree. He tested the knot twice to be sure it would hold.

"Come over here, fella. Come here, Tiny," Jason

called. He clapped his hands and whistled to get Tiny's attention.

"Maybe after you teach him to come, you can teach him to roll over," Eddie said as Tiny trampled toward where Jason was ruffling leaves to show Tiny where to bed down. "He looks pretty smart. You might get him to fetch or count to ten like a trick horse I saw once on TV."

Jason nodded. "Yeah, Tiny does seem smarter than most animals. How do you think he'd do on a book report?"

Jason spread his T-shirt out like a pillow and waited. Tiny was whining again.

Together, the boys rubbed the baby mastodon's back and shoulders, trying to calm him. Using their fingers, they combed through Tiny's rough red fur and the delicate golden hairs underneath. They tickled the soft spot under Tiny's chin.

"Shhh," Jason put his finger to his lips as the baby mastodon sank down in the leaves and fell asleep.

"You think he'll be OK?" Eddie whispered as they tiptoed through the woods.

"Yeah," Jason kept his voice low. "Nobody ever comes back here except us."

"But what if he makes that trumpeting noise like he made in your living room?"

"He won't," Jason answered. "He's asleep. Even if he did, nobody would hear. See you in the morning. Early," he added, in case Eddie wanted to sleep till noon. "And remember, you can't tell anybody—none of the kids from school. If the phone rings, don't even go near it." Jason put his face next to Eddie's. "And don't tell your dad either, and especially not your mom."

"I know, I know. You don't have to keep reminding me."

"You can't tell *anybody!* I'm not telling anybody either. How many people do you know who could keep something like Tiny a secret? The next thing you know, Tiny would be . . . well, you know. He'd either be stuffed and put in the Smithsonian or he'd be like those baby monkeys I was telling you about."

"I wouldn't have a chance to tell my parents anyway," Eddie said. "When my mom comes home from the Million Dollar Club, she doesn't want to be bothered with kid stuff. She's too busy phoning everyone who wasn't there. That takes half the night. I'll be asleep when my dad comes in. If Nana was still living with us, I could tell her."

Nana was Eddie's grandmother. She used to make them peanut-butter cookies and cupcakes with little messages tucked inside. When Nana died, Jason's mom had let him miss school to go to the funeral.

Jason cleared his throat. "If you have to tell someone, call me."

"It'll never happen. My mom will be on the phone, remember?"

After giving Eddie a thumbs-up, Jason hurried through the back door and into the kitchen, being careful the storm door didn't slam behind him. His parents were still in the living room.

Wasting no time, Jason walked up the steps to his bedroom, where he stripped off his clothes and kicked them under his bed. When his mom came up later to kiss him good night, he didn't want her to see the red hairs. That was another thing he was learning about mastodons. They shed like crazy.

Jason climbed into bed and turned off the light. In a million years, he never would have expected it to be so hard leaving a pet alone in the woods. It felt worse than when his mom first got her job at Smith, Beazley, and Berg. Coming home to an empty house was like the end of the world. It was lonelier than he'd ever imagined. At least he'd had Brandy. Poor Tiny, Jason thought. He didn't have anybody.

Jason's feet hit the floor and he rushed to the window. Whew! As much as he longed to see Tiny's soulful green eyes, his curling red trunk, and thick mat of hair, Jason was relieved when he could not. If he couldn't spot Tiny from where he stood, then nobody else could either. For the time being, Tiny was safe.

Jason climbed back into bed. He was tired from raking, he was exhausted from worry, but he was still too restless to sleep. Finally, out of desperation, Jason turned on the lamp beside his bed. Right away his eyes fell on the book his father had left on the nightstand.

Slowly he picked it up. One chapter should put him right to sleep. The last thing Jason remembered was being amazed by the girl, Julie, alone on the tundra with nothing but her wits to help her survive. If only he could ask her: How am I ever going to mow, rake, and haul two *tons* of grass?

The next afternoon Eddie pointed out another problem.

"You've got to do something, Jason," Eddie said, swatting a fly off his arm.

Jason thoughtfully shifted his baseball cap.

"About what?" he asked.

"About all this stuff lying around." Eddie pointed to a pile of mastodon dung.

"Like what?"

"How the heck should I know?" Eddie sniffled and sneezed. The flies and summer's heat were making Eddie's temper short. "Maybe you should sell it. My mother says people will buy anything if you talk to them long enough. I tell you, you've got to think of something. Last night when I was baby-sitting Tiny while you were eating dinner, I dozed off. When I woke up, there was a fly crawling up my nose as big as a June bug. We've got to do something with all this manure."

"OK," Jason said reluctantly. He'd been hoping that if he waited long enough, the manure would disappear on its own.

"Well?" Eddie snapped. He took a handkerchief out of his pocket.

"We'll sell it to people to spread on their lawns and

gardens." Jason started for the shed, although he wasn't in much of a rush. He'd already been through the neighborhood, raking grass clippings. He'd made two trips before returning *Julie of the Wolves* to the library. Now, thanks to Eddie, he was taking out the wheelbarrow again.

"Maybe this isn't such a hot idea after all," Eddie said. "Something tells me we can't go through the neighborhood one time raking up grass clippings, the next time selling manure."

"You got a better one?" Jason snapped. He dropped a heavy shovelful into the wheelbarrow.

As though he'd picked up on the tension in the boys' voices, Tiny looked up from nibbling a small fir tree. *Thud, thud, thud, thud.* He ambled over to stand shyly behind Jason. Hooking his chin on Jason's shoulder, he timidly extended his trunk toward Eddie.

Jason looked at Eddie and smiled. "The little guy likes us."

"I don't know about the 'little' part, but he likes us, sure enough."

At the sound of Eddie's voice, Tiny's eyes blinked. Once, twice. Slow and dreamy.

Eddie put his arms around Tiny's neck and rested his head against the mastodon's furry shoulder. The three of them stood there for the longest time, just being together.

More than anything, Jason wished it could always be like this. But what was the chance of that?

Chapter 6

Words Overheard

That evening Jason was in the kitchen, spreading thick globs of peanut butter across slices of white bread. He peeked into the living room, where his parents were watching TV.

"Hey, that's Eddie's mother!" he screamed as the knife clattered to the floor.

How embarrassing for Eddie. There was Mrs. Huddleston with a bunch of other women, carrying signs and marching back and forth in front of a house that looked vaguely familiar.

Jason felt his eyes almost pop out of his head. They were picketing Gamma Rays's house!

Lucky for Jason, his mother was too busy working to do anything rude like that.

A new idea struck Jason. What if the reporters who were covering Mrs. Huddleston's neighborhood protest decided to take a nice relaxing walk through the woods? What if they found Tiny?

Jason scowled. Why couldn't Eddie keep his mother inside? It was hard enough trying to figure out how to feed a mastodon. He'd never been so exhausted in his life. Now, thanks to Eddie's mother, he had to worry about a bunch of snoopy reporters.

His head pounding from lack of sleep, Jason went back to slapping peanut butter on bread. He watched anxiously as his mother set her newspaper aside. "Let's see if Marge is on the other channels."

"I would but I can't seem to locate the remote." Jason held his breath as his father bent over the couch and tossed the cushions on the floor. "It was definitely here Sunday night. I know because I used it."

"You're lucky it worked," Mrs. Richards said. "It was broken when you were out of town."

"How could it be broken? It was practically brand new."

"I don't know how. And don't blame the kids, because you use that remote as much as anyone." Jason loved it when his mother said things like that. "All I know is whenever I changed channels, instead of getting a local station, I got sumo wrestlers from Japan."

"Probably one of those morning talk shows."

"Excuse me! This was late at night, and I think I stayed home long enough taking care of Jason and Brandy to recognize what a talk show looks like."

Hearing his name, Jason stopped what he was doing and listened more closely. "I figured we were still having problems with the antenna," his mother went on. "Remember how you and Jason tried to straighten it after that last storm? Anyway, I bumped into Mr. Gammel at Radio Shack."

"Gammel? Why do we have to run to him every time we have a problem with the TV?"

Mom let out a loud sigh. "Because I don't like you fooling around with antennas, which you know nothing about. You ought to be grateful to Mr. Gammel for connecting that little receiver box to our television. You have to admit it helped for a while. I honestly think that man is a genius."

"Because he connected one little electrical box to the TV set? You're lucky he didn't blow it up."

"Don't be ridiculous. Anyway, according to Mr. Gammel, the problem wasn't our antenna. Our remote wasn't strong enough to work with that new high-tech receiver he gave us. Whatever he did to the remote certainly helped. We stopped getting those sumo wrestlers. Of course, we still had those strange flickerings behind the TV screen."

Mr. Richards replaced the last cushion on the couch. "That's exactly why we have to get rid of that satellite dish. It's destroying our TV reception. No matter what your so-called genius says or does, he's still responsible for ruining the television reception in our neighborhood." Mr. Richards stopped abruptly as something else seemed to come to mind.

Meanwhile, Jason was dumping the sandwiches in a bag.

"By the way," his father said. "I saw Mr. Gammel when I was bringing the trash cans in off the street. He wanted to know if Jason had joined the circus. Can you beat that? Something about grass clippings and elephant poop."

Jason folded the bag. He lifted it off the counter and started walking slowly toward the door.

"I, for one, would like to hear Jason's explanation," his father went on. "And what about his reading?"

"He went to the library," Jason's mother offered. "Brandy thinks he reads in the bathtub."

"He took a bath without being told?" Mr. Richards sounded stunned. "He's not interested in girls yet, is he?"

"I hope not. One lovesick child at a time is enough. I don't think Brandy left her room all day. She's up there now staring at the phone, waiting for that boy who works at McDonald's to call."

Quiet. Quiet. It was important the floor didn't creak. Jason knew what was going to happen next.

"Where is Jason? Jason!" his father called.

Jason quietly closed the door. Head down, feet pumping, he raced toward the woods with his bag of peanut-butter-and-jelly sandwiches. Why had Gamma Rays been watching him? All he'd been doing was raking lawns and selling manure.

The answer didn't come until Jason stopped running, but when it did, it hit him like a ton of bricks. Their houses were on the same side of the street. Gamma Rays's property backed up to the woods too. What if Gamma Rays had seen him and Eddie sneaking back and forth and decided to explore the woods for himself? What if Gamma Rays had taken a photograph of Tiny?

Images of scientists wearing white coats and brandishing foot-long hypodermic needles swam in front of Jason's eyes as he collapsed on the log next to Eddie.

"We've got a big problem," Jason panted as he handed Eddie the sandwiches.

"Yeah, really big. Look at him." Eddie pointed his thumb at Tiny. "When he got here yesterday, he was up to my chest. Now he's up to my nose. We can't hide something like this forever. We've got to do something, Jase. Quick!"

Chapter 7

Keeping Secrets

"Stop bugging me. As soon as I get some sleep, I *am* going to do something," Jason snapped. "It's too late tonight, but first thing tomorrow, I'm going to check out Mr. Gammel."

Eddie's eyes almost flew out of his head.

"Gamma Rays? That maniac?" Eddie yelped. He leaned the pitchfork against a tree.

"I told you"—Jason needed something to do with his hands, so he grabbed the pitchfork and began pitching grass to Tiny for his evening snack—"Gamma Rays has been spying on me. What if he's got pictures? What if he tells?"

"Whoa! You don't exactly go trooping through the neighborhood hauling manure and not have people notice."

"I still say we've got to find out if he knows anything about Tiny."

"And if he does know, then what?"

"We move him."

"Who?"

"Tiny. We find another place to hide him."

"Yeah, right," Eddie said sarcastically. "We spend the whole summer and maybe the rest of our lives leading Tiny around the woods on a leash so nobody can find him. Meanwhile, Tiny is growing and eating everything in sight. Get real, Jase. Sometime, someplace, somebody's going to find out. If it's not Gamma Rays, it'll be somebody else."

"I told you," Jason insisted. "We can't let anything bad happen to Tiny." Yawning, Jason plopped down on the log. "But the only way to find out if Gamma Rays knows anything is if I knock on his door and ask him."

Eddie took a handkerchief out of his pocket and blew his nose a couple of times. Wearily, he turned back to Jason.

"Did you already forget how Mr. Gammel is practically wrecking the neighborhood? I tell you, the man's crazy. He puts a silver satellite dish in his front yard, when everybody knows that's not allowed. The guy's a regular renegade. That's what my mom says. A crackpot."

"What your mom says doesn't count," Jason said. "She's in real estate. She just wants Gamma Rays to move so she can sell his house." The moment the words left his mouth, Jason was sorry. Nobody likes to hear something mean said about his or her mom.

"That's a rotten thing to say." Eddie stood up, hands on hips, his face growing as red as a tomato. "At least my mom cares about what happens in our neighborhood. That's a lot more than some moms do. If your mom cared, she'd join my mom's committee."

"Huh." Jason stood up and walked over to Tiny. Nobody was going to say anything bad about *Jason's* mother and get away with it. Not even Eddie. "Maybe my mom doesn't think it's such a great idea to take TV away from an old man. It's not his fault he's weird."

"It's not the TV set. It's that satellite dish!" Eddie yelled.

Jason scratched the wrinkle behind Tiny's ear to keep him calm. He ran his fingers through the tangle of red hair as Tiny raised his head and searched Jason's face. It made Jason feel awful. You'd think he and Eddie would have more sense than to fight about their mothers in front of Tiny. Tiny's mom was probably bawling her eyes out, wondering what had happened to her baby, just like the mother in *Dumbo*.

In the distance, night birds were calling their mates. Jason motioned for Tiny to lie down. Leaves rustled and a rabbit scooted through the clearing. Jason barely noticed, he was so exhausted. The shadows had long disappeared when Tiny's head sank deep into the bed of pine needles and oak leaves. Jason sat watching Tiny's side breathe in and out.

When Jason glanced up, Eddie was starting to sneeze. "Shhh."

Eddie caught himself in time.

Jason didn't feel comfortable talking until they were safely out of the clearing and leaning against the back of his house. "I guess we're more tired than I thought," he said, yawning. "Still friends?"

"Yeah." Eddie smiled.

"We can't let Gamma Rays or anybody find out," Jason said. "Tiny trusts us."

Eddie rubbed his eye with his finger. "I don't like this secrecy stuff. Just because Tiny didn't show up wearing a collar doesn't mean he doesn't belong to someone. And even if he doesn't, there's probably a law against hiding mastodons. And you know something else?"

Jason was almost afraid to ask.

"You keep saying how you don't want Tiny to be turned into an experiment but I bet you never thought he might already be an experiment. Maybe he escaped from some laboratory and right now a bunch of scientists in white coats are prowling around looking for him. Here he is, a zillion-dollar scientific marvel, and we're hiding him in the woods! Jason, I tell you. We'll get sent to jail."

What a thing to say.

Just then a yellow light flicked on in Brandy's room. Brandy opened her window and stuck her head out.

I want you, I need you.

"Jason? Is that you down there?" She had to yell so Jason could hear her over the stereo.

I love you with all my heart.

"Who were you expecting? Your burger babe?" Jason yelled back.

"Shut up, bird brain!" Brandy slammed the window down.

Jason turned to Eddie. "Hey, I'm not going to do anything stupid enough to land us in jail. But if anybody knows about people running around in white coats or missing baby mastodons, it might be Gamma Rays. Tomorrow I'm going over to his house, and don't try to stop me. We've got to find out exactly what he knows about Tiny."

Chapter 8

The Peculiar Mr. Gamma Rays

Sometimes Jason had to give Brandy credit. She was like a juggler he'd seen on TV. The juggler was throwing chairs, watermelons, and chainsaws and catching every one. Brandy didn't exactly throw chainsaws, but she could do more things at the same time than anyone else Jason had ever known. Right now, Brandy was upstairs sitting on her bed with little white balls of cotton stuffed between her toes, painting her toenails with a color that would stop traffic. She was also listening to Elvis wailing about suspicious minds and being caught in a trap with one ear while growing a telephone out of the other.

What she was saying didn't make much sense. But then what could you expect from a girl?

"DeeDee said that Karen said that she saw *mumble whisper mumble mumble* at McDonald's."

Pause.

"Nooooo. She saw *that?*"

Pause.

"You saw him *what?*" followed by an ear-splitting shriek.

Down slammed the phone.

Jason was in the living room, staring out the window. He was thinking about the juggler and how, right now, catching a chainsaw seemed simple compared to what he had to do next: go over to see good old Mr. Gamma Rays.

Last October when Gamma Rays had moved into the neighborhood, Jason and Eddie sat on the curb and watched everything being unloaded from the van. They'd hoped for bicycles, skateboards, bunk beds, or anything that hinted of kids. No such luck. Instead there was the normal couch, chairs, dining room table. Boring stuff. But then came the trunks, big black steel trunks, the kind that, if larger, might have been coffins. Watching, Eddie's eyes had almost popped out of his head. Jason choked on his gum.

They were still sitting on the curb, too awestruck to leave, when the movers rolled the empty wheelchair down the ramp and into the house.

It was later that night, after Jason's mother returned from taking a casserole over to welcome their new neighbors, that Jason learned Gamma Rays was a photographer-turned-inventor who used to work for *National Geographic*. The trunks were for his camera gear. The wheelchair was for his invalid mother.

What could be scary about an old man and his even older mother? Just because someone had seen a laser gun, which Jason's mother said was a harmless invention for retouching photographs, that was no reason to be scared.

But if Gamma Rays was harmless, then how come Eddie's mom called him a maniac? Why did Jason's dad say Gamma Rays and his satellite dish posed a threat to the entire neighborhood?

Jason headed down the street toward Gamma Rays's house. He'd find out soon enough.

Jason tried to clear his throat as he pressed his finger to the doorbell, but he was too nervous. Probably he was getting ready to have a heart attack. When Gamma Rays finally opened the door, Jason would be crumpled in a heap.

Jason could see the headline: BOY FOUND DEADER THAN A DOORKNOB.

When Jason caught himself biting the skin around his thumbnail, he quickly tucked his hand under his arm, trying to look casual. The headline changed: TEN-YEAR-OLD BOY DIES WITHOUT A THUMB TO HIS NAME.

Now he was biting his lip instead. Jason swallowed. If only he could keep his teeth still.

LIPLESS TEN-YEAR-OLD DISCOVERED DEAD.

Oh, what was the use? There was no use beating around the bush. He should just say, "Seen any good mastodons lately?"

Jason knew what he *should* be doing. He *should* be reading a book. If he didn't finish two books by the end of the week, his parents would ground him for sure. Then who would take care of Tiny? Eddie couldn't do it by himself.

That wasn't the only thing that bothered Jason.

If Gamma Rays was about to turn Tiny into a scientific experiment, or worse, if Tiny *was* his scientific experiment . . . Jason's teeth rattled with nervousness.

If it wasn't for Tiny, Jason would run right now.

Jason rang the bell again.

"Boy!"

Jason almost flew out of his skin as Gamma Rays loomed in front of him.

"Don't just stand there, boy." Gamma Rays clicked a pair of tongs over Jason's head. "Quick! Whatever it is you're selling, you'll have to tell me in the dark."

Jason sucked in his breath as Gamma Rays turned on his heel and, waving the tongs in the air, headed for what Jason assumed was the basement.

"But, wait! I'm not selling . . . I just wanted to ask . . ." Jason bounded down the steps after Gamma Rays, stopping short as the man disappeared behind a long black curtain.

"Where are you, boy?"

"Right behind you, sir," Jason gulped. Except for a red lightbulb dangling in a corner, everything was as black as night.

Slowly Jason's eyes became accustomed to the darkness. Gamma Rays was working in front of a long narrow table with his back to Jason. To his left stood something that looked like an X-ray machine. To his right were three smelly trays.

He never should have come here alone and without telling his parents.

Muttering under his breath, Gamma Rays slipped a sheet of paper out of a box and slid it under the machine. He picked a metal object off the table.

The laser gun!

Jason's voice caught in his throat. "My mom said you had an invention."

"Ah, recognition!" Gamma Rays motioned with his head, signaling for Jason to come still closer. "I could use some help. You ever work in a darkroom?"

"Not really."

"Didn't think so. You're too nervous. You have a camera?" When he tapped the tongs on the edge of the tray, Jason jumped.

"I did," Jason answered, anxious to see if Gamma Rays was working on a picture of Tiny. "I got a camera for my birthday once, but I left it outside and it rained."

"Here." Before Jason could take a step backward, Gamma Rays grabbed his arm. "Tilt the tray with this hand. Hold the tongs with your other hand and keep the print moving in the solution. You can flip it over now. Easy. Easy."

Gamma Rays seemed unaware of how Jason's heart kept crashing like a cymbal in his chest. "Catch the print by the corner. You'll have to transfer it to the second tray and then the third when I tell you."

Jason's mind reeled. If it *was* a picture of Tiny, why would Gamma Rays want him to know he knew, unless . . . Jason shuddered.

Behind him, Gamma Rays was clipping black crinkly strips to metal coat hangers. Jason didn't dare think of the danger he might be in. Instead he peered closer as the print came into focus.

There was a faint outline of . . . a television set? Jason leaned forward, struggling to see through the dim red light as the images inside the television set gradually grew sharper.

It wasn't Tiny.

It was a puppet on strings. A boy puppet with freckles and a smiling face. He was wearing a plaid shirt with a bandanna and cowboy boots.

Gamma Rays didn't flick on the brighter overhead light until the print was soaking in the third tray.

"I simply can't understand how . . ." Shoulders hunched forward, Gamma Rays nudged Jason through the black curtains and into the main area of the basement.

Quickly Jason scanned the room. He didn't relax until he spotted the set of sliding glass doors leading to the backyard. If he had to, he could make a speedy exit.

What he needed was to get the information he'd come for and then leave. Somehow he had to casually bring up the subject of mastodons. Otherwise, he and Eddie had decided, it would arouse suspicion.

"For a second I thought that photograph might be a mastodon," Jason said slowly. Okay, so maybe it sounded crazy, but what did he care. "I thought you had a picture of a mastodon."

"A mastodon!"

Jason jumped. Gamma Rays began to pace wildly about the room.

"Ah, the magnificent Ice Age beast!" Gamma Rays shouted. "One of the most curious creatures ever to inhabit this earth! That is until our early ancestors killed them off. Meat on the table, furs on the ladies! Some things never change!"

"I mean . . ." Jason gulped. "Do you know if there ever were any mastodons around *here*?"

The question was Eddie's idea. In a roundabout way, it was supposed to tell them if Gamma Rays knew anything about Tiny. The way the boys figured it, there were two things they needed to find out. First, they needed to know if Gamma Rays knew anything at all about Tiny. If he didn't, then they needed to know how Tiny might have appeared in the Richards's family room.

"Around *here*," Jason repeated. He waited anxiously for Gamma Rays's answer.

"Well, now, let's see." Gamma Rays rocked back on

his heels. He rubbed his chin thoughtfully. "Ah, yes. This would have been during the Pleistocene period or the Great Ice Age. That was fifty to seventy thousand years ago, when the world was more like a giant snowball and colder than a—Take my word for it. Cold."

He paused, eyes narrowed on Jason. "There is evidence of mastodon migration across the Great Plains. They also apparently lived in California, Florida, and Texas. I believe a tooth of a giant mastodon was found in New York, but nothing was ever found here in this neck of the woods."

"Maybe the mastodon wouldn't have lived . . . here," Jason began cautiously. "But what if, a long time ago, a mastodon got separated from its family while they were roaming the Great Plains. Kids get lost all the time. It could happen to a mastodon. Like, what if a baby mastodon fell into a snowdrift or something? The mother wouldn't be able to find it then. And maybe the baby just now dug itself out or got melted or something. And maybe, after it woke up, it took a little walk and ended up here. I saw in a movie once how it happened to a caveman. So, could it happen to a mastodon?"

Gamma Rays pinched his lip with his finger, obviously concentrating very hard on Jason's question. "Still alive?"

Just then a bell rang upstairs.

"You'll have to excuse me. It's 'Howdy Doody' time," Gamma Rays said, tapping on his watch.

" 'Howdy Doody'? What's that?"

A shadow flittered briefly across Gamma Rays's face. "Oh, yes." He smiled bashfully. "You're too young to know about Howdy. It's a children's program from back in the fifties. Curious that I'm tuning it in live today. Whatever. Mother likes it. The picture you printed— that was Howdy Doody. Cheerful little fellow! Usually soccer games out of Australia and sumo wrestling from Japan keep Mother's blood pumping, but every once in a while she wants the satellite dish adjusted so she can hook into 'Howdy Doody.' I don't know what we'll do if we're forced to take our satellite dish down."

Gamma Rays scrambled up the steps, two at a time.

"Wait," Jason shouted. "What about the mastodons?"

"Help yourself. Make yourself at home. There are photo albums in the bookcase," Gamma Rays called from somewhere upstairs. "You can let yourself out when you're finished."

Jason blinked with surprise. Help yourself? Unsupervised? He glanced around the room, noticing for the first time the bookshelves crammed floor to ceiling, the desk with its computer equipment, and the souvenirs Gamma Rays had apparently brought back from his many travels.

Okay, so Gamma Rays knew him, sort of. He knew Jason's father enough to ask if his son had joined the circus. He knew Jason's mom enough to eat her cooking and fix their TV. Even so, Jason didn't know many grown-ups who would trust him in their basement alone.

Jason walked slowly around the desk and eased an album out of the bookcase. He was pretty sure it wouldn't be like the photo albums his mom had at home. He could already see that instead of three small snapshots to a page, there was only one big photograph in a plastic sleeve.

Jason turned the pages. Anacondas, alligators, dolphins, whales. They'd studied endangered species in school.

Jason pulled other albums off the shelf. Here were fiery rockets and pictures of planets obviously shot through powerful telescopic lenses. For a moment, he almost forgot about Tiny. Judging by the photographs, there was nothing Gamma Rays hadn't seen.

Meanwhile, muffled sounds floated down from the room above Jason's head: *mumble . . . mumble . . . summer fall winter spring . . . mumble . . . mumble.* Jason cocked his head at the sound of a squeaking bicycle horn followed by children's laughter.

Satisfied, Jason shut the last album and placed it back in the bookcase. He left quietly.

As far as he could tell, Gamma Rays didn't know anything about Tiny. Still, as Jason crossed through the back lawn and headed toward the woods where Eddie would be anxiously waiting, there was something that kept nagging at the back of his mind.

What was it?

Chapter 9

The Search Begins

"I tell you, Eddie. The man has been everyplace. The pyramids. The rain forests. He had fantastic pictures of every endangered species you'd ever want to think about. Snow leopards, polar bears, owls. You should have seen the neat one of the blue whales."

They were taking turns raking the scattered grass clippings.

Eddie rolled his eyes and groaned as Jason went on.

"I bet he knows *every*thing about *every*thing. I bet he's a regular walking, talking encyclopedia. If he was a teacher, we wouldn't even have to bother with college. We'd learn everything we ever needed to know in fifth grade."

"Except you can't trust him," Eddie said. "Not with those cameras and that computer and that satellite dish. He's probably a spy."

Jason sighed. "Give me a break. He takes pictures of puppets on a television set. And his mother watches soccer and sumo wrestling. I just wish I'd had a chance to ask him more questions about mastodons. You think I ought to check out the library?"

Eddie shrugged. "You've got to do something. You want me to go along?"

"What, and leave Tiny! No, you stay here. Someone has to."

Eddie shook his head in disgust. "Jase, staying here once in a while is okay, but I'm not a nanny."

Just then, music Jason would recognize anywhere filtered through the woods. Hearing Elvis Presley, he knew Brandy couldn't be far behind.

If you can't come around me
at least please telephone . . .

"What's that?" Obviously, Eddie wasn't as familiar with Elvis Presley as Jason was. Let Eddie live in the same house as Brandy, and he'd get acquainted real quick.

Quickly Jason headed along the narrow path. At the edge of the woods, he knelt down. Eddie knelt beside him.

Brandy's boom box, with Elvis twanging away, was positioned next to a lawn chair. Brandy was dragging the plastic wading pool left over from Jason's childhood to the middle of the yard. She was wearing her swimsuit.

Eddie picked up his binoculars and leaned forward as

Brandy turned around and walked barefoot back toward the house. Next she dragged the hose over and filled the wading pool.

Baby, it's just you I'm thinking of.

No doubt about it: Brandy had lost all her marbles. Nobody could swim laps in a wading pool.

"She's taking the hose back now," Eddie whispered in case Jason couldn't see.

"Now she's climbing in. She's lying down. Faceup."

It was true. Brandy was lying in the little round wading pool. All Jason could see was the top of her head, her blond hair hanging over the edge, and, on the other end, the tips of her toes with red nail polish sticking straight up like stop signs.

Jason couldn't stand it any longer. He walked into the yard, whistling nonchalantly. If Brandy bothered to ask, he would tell her the truth. He would say he was passing by on his way to the library.

Even for Brandy, this was weird. She was lying on the sea horses painted on the bottom of the pool. It looked like one of them was nibbling on her ear. Her arms were spread out. One hand was holding a can of cola. Her eyes were shut. Meanwhile, Elvis was singing "Heartbreak Hotel."

I get so lonely, get so lonely . . .

"Brandy, what do you think you're doing?"
Brandy's eyes flew open.

"Get away, creep. You're making a shadow! I'm getting a suntan, or I was until you blocked every single ray in the entire universe. Kindly move your bod about five miles in either direction."

"You're going to get burned. What number sunscreen do you have on?"

"What are you, my mother? Now scram."

"You're supposed to be by the phone in case Mom calls."

Brandy cupped one hand over her eyes like a visor and gestured with the other. "Cordless."

Of course.

Jason knew what the problem was. He'd heard her moaning and groaning and stomping around the house, slamming cabinets, all because the great McDonald's burger flipper was making goo-goo eyes at some other blonde from another school. How ridiculous. That was the thing about girls. They were too possessive. A guy couldn't even talk to someone else without the world crashing around his head.

Jason was glad he was a guy. With guys it was different. Just because he thought Gamma Rays was the most brilliant person he'd ever met in his life, you didn't hear Eddie . . . Jason stopped, recalling the peculiar way Eddie had been behaving.

Was Eddie jealous? Jason wondered as he headed toward the library. Maybe guys and girls weren't so different after all.

* * *

A few minutes later, Jason sat down in front of the computer at the library. It would tell him where to find the stuff he needed. He'd watched someone else do it. No way was he going to ask a librarian for help. He knew librarians from school. They always asked tricky questions. In two seconds, they'd know he had a live mastodon in his backyard.

Jason tapped the keyboard. The screen filled with words.

Oh, no! Tiny was in more danger than he'd ever imagined. The first book on the list was called *Mastodon Hunters,* and it was five hundred and sixty-five pages long. That's a lot of hunters!

Now that he knew where to look, Jason hurried over to the shelves. He could hardly believe his eyes. Four whole shelves and over a hundred books on dinosaurs, but only five measly books that told anything about mastodons. Unfair! If he was Tiny, his feelings would be hurt!

If only people knew how mastodons could take the tip of their trunk and curl it like a finger. If only people knew how they could rub against you, gentle as a kitten, or play tug of war, playful as a puppy. No, Jason reminded himself. He wasn't about to tell anybody.

Finally Jason checked out the two books with the most interesting pictures. He tucked them under his arm and carried them home.

Chapter 10

The Mysterious Mastodon

"Look at this! A beaver as big as a bear!" Jason was sitting on a log, bent over a book, while Eddie used a pitchfork to rearrange piles of grass clippings. Some of the grass was already starting to ferment. If Tiny got an upset stomach, they'd have even bigger problems.

"Did you know there used to be prehistoric rhinos too? I wonder why Gamma Rays didn't mention— Yikes! Saber-tooth tigers. Wait. Here, it tells about Tiny."

Jason read the words out loud, glancing up occasionally to be sure he had Eddie's attention.

" 'The imperial mastodon was, at its largest, fourteen feet at the shoulder with tusks more than twelve feet long. It weighed six tons.' "

Eddie lifted another batch of grass clippings from the bottom of a pile and set the clippings on the top.

"Yeah, colossal. Look at him. Like I said, Jason, we can't hide something this big forever."

Jason read on. "'In the summer, the mastodon ate grass. In the winter, it swept away snow with its tusks to find grass underneath.' I bet Gamma Rays knows all this. He just couldn't blab about everything because of his mother and 'Howdy Doody' time."

"*Yeee-augggghhhhhh.*" Eddie stepped back. He wiped his nose with his arm. "Speaking of grass, did I tell you I might be developing an allergy?" He sniffed and then sneezed. "When I'm not sneezing, my nose runs. When my nose isn't running, my eyes sting. And I itch all over. Jase, you better decide what we're going to do."

Jason was too absorbed in the book to listen to Eddie's tirade. Instead of responding, Jason waved absently with his hand. "Wait a sec. I'm finding out . . . It says here . . . I wonder if Gamma . . . something about some mystery or something."

"Hah." Thoroughly disgusted, Eddie threw the pitchfork on the ground. He stomped over to stand an inch in front of Jason's toe and hollered so loud, his ears turned red.

"Forget the great and awesome Gamma Rays!" Eddie shouted. "The only thing I want to know is what's going to happen if Tiny doesn't get enough to eat. He looks tame enough now, but what if he gets those twelve-foot tusks? What if he eats every leaf and blade of grass in this whole neighborhood?"

Eddie wiped the sweat off his forehead. "I don't know about you, Jase, but I don't exactly want to wind up being a mastodon's last meal. Look at him!"

Tiny was ignoring the grass Eddie had thoughtfully set close by. Instead the mastodon was busy pulling pine trees up by their roots. He thrashed them on the ground to loosen the soil, then devoured them—roots, cones, needles, and all.

"Hey, here it is." Jason's face lit up. He pointed to a paragraph in the book.

Eddie plopped down on the log beside Jason and started reading too. He stopped to whistle, long and low. "Wow. So nobody knows what happened to the mastodons. Not even your great know-it-all genius, Mr. Gamma Rays."

One good thing—maybe the only good thing—about having Brandy for a sister was that Jason had learned how to let certain things go. Eddie's wise remarks went in one ear and out the other.

"If only Tiny could tell us," Jason mused out loud.

"So," Eddie said, clearing his throat. "As long as certain people keep Tiny to themselves, no one will ever know the answer." Eddie stood up. After making a big production out of dusting the grass off his pants, he started to pace. Finally, just when Jason thought he might dig a trench out of the path he'd created, Eddie stopped. He crossed his arms and put one foot on the log next to where Jason was sitting.

"Maybe," Eddie said, sounding very methodical, "we

shouldn't keep the world's last surviving mastodon a secret. Like it says in the book, the key to the mystery is important. A cosmic problem. We could be on the brink of another ice age. We've got to tell. Maybe we could find an animal-rights group or a bunch of rangers, somebody who would protect Tiny."

For a second, the bit about the cosmic problem almost had Jason convinced. But what Eddie said next was enough to make Jason puke.

"What do you think he's worth? Not that we'd sell him. But he has to be worth something."

"Are you crazy?" Jason said. "I thought you liked Tiny."

Eddie wasn't listening.

"When my mom sells a house, she checks a computer to see what other houses are going for. It has to do with the market. So when it comes to mastodons," Eddie said, "what do you think the market will bear?"

"Stop!"

Jason watched in horror as Eddie walked closer to where Tiny was feeding.

"Not even in the name of science? A million. Maybe a million and a half."

"Are you nuts?" Jason screamed. "Are you forgetting what happened to ET?"

"Hey," Eddie's eyes were the size of Ping-Pong balls. "You think we could train him? He'd be great for commercials. You know the commercial where it's snowing really hard and the alarm goes off in this guy's house because he's the doctor and he's got to deliver a baby, only his car won't start because the battery died? Well, picture this, Jase. Instead of a car, the doctor has a mastodon waiting in the garage—Tiny, of course—to take him to the hospital. You think the battery people would like that?"

Eddie wasn't finished. "How about the commercial where the guys are sitting around a table playing cards and one of the guys wants a soda, so his dog goes to the refrigerator and brings it back? Instead of the dog, what if it was Tiny?"

Eddie was on a roll. "I tell you, we have got to stop worrying about how Tiny got here and start thinking about what we're going to do with him. I say we turn Tiny into a television star."

Jason stood up slowly and stared straight into Eddie's eyes. It took everything he had not to slam his fist into Eddie's shoulder.

"No, no, NO!" Jason yelled. "We're not going to sell and we're not going to *tell* either."

As Eddie stepped closer, Jason's eyes turned steely.

"Not for a million dollars?" Eddie shouted. "Your mother could quit her job. Your dad could get that lawn service he's always wanted. Think how important you'd be. Rich and famous too."

For a split second Jason's mind whirled. Brandy could have her own phone line. He and Eddie could buy matching red Lamborghini sports cars.

Then Jason glanced at the baby mastodon, who was busy exploring a line of ants with his trunk. It wasn't fair. A kid shouldn't have to make such tough decisions.

"Important?" Jason said with disgust. "We're *responsible* for Tiny. How do you think I feel seeing him tied up like this? Tiny doesn't belong here and he knows it. If we can find out how Tiny got here, maybe we can send him back. We can't sell out now. Not even for a million dollars!"

Eddie plopped down on the edge of the log. He propped his elbows on his knees and rested his head between his hands. He was frowning because he wished it wasn't so easy for his friend to give up a million dollars.

"No offense, Jase," he said finally, "but anybody else who found Tiny wouldn't think twice about cashing in. You can't keep putting it off. Every day you try to keep Tiny a secret, he gets that much closer to being found out. And when it comes to a million dollars, I don't think there's many people you can trust."

It wasn't what Jason wanted to hear, but he knew Eddie was right.

Chapter 11

Brandy's Big Mouth

Jason finished both library books that same afternoon. The first book told all about mastodons. The second explained how the world had changed from the Great Ice Age to the present because of human pollution and lack of respect for the environment. The problem was, neither book revealed how Tiny had appeared in Jason's living room or how Jason could get the baby mastodon back to his mother where he really belonged.

After dinner, Jason was staring out his bedroom window. The sun was sinking fast. So was Jason's heart. In the background Elvis was belting out something about peace and understanding. Right, Elvis. Sometime.

Jason was convinced it was only a matter of time before Eddie caved in. It was only because of their friendship that Eddie had lasted this long. He couldn't exactly blame Eddie. What could you expect from a kid with a mother who belonged to a Million Dollar Club and a father who bowled for dollars? Jason was beginning to understand why whenever they played Monopoly, Eddie always had to be the banker.

Jason was thinking there had to be something he could do when he heard Brandy arguing with Mom. Jason's ears perked up right away. Nobody could change Jason's mood faster than Brandy, and right now his mood definitely needed improvement. Jason tiptoed across the room and opened his bedroom door.

"I still don't see why I have to stay here while you and Dad go out," Brandy was saying. "All I want to do is go to McDonald's with DeeDee."

"Darling, when your young man is ready to call, he'll call. He probably tried and the line was busy."

"We have call waiting, remember? By the time he gets around to calling me, he'll be married and have ten kids."

"Sounds like a hamster."

"Mother, that's not funny."

"I know, sweetheart. I know you don't believe this, but I do remember what it was like to be fifteen and in love."

"You didn't fall in love until you met Dad. That doesn't count. Dad doesn't even have all of his hair, and besides, that was back in the Dark Ages. They probably didn't even have telephones back then."

"I remember standing on a hill and waiting for a smoke signal."

"Mother!"

"It was a windy day."

"Mother!"

"And then a big dark cloud came whooshing across the sky."

"Mother!"

"The cloud opened up. And it rained."

By now, Jason was rolling on the floor, doubled up with laughter. His mother really knew how to handle Brandy.

"You are the most insensitive person I know," Brandy yelled. "You aren't even human! You don't care!"

Jason would never admit it, but he really admired the fact that his sister would stoop to anything to get what she wanted. She was one of the most stubborn people Jason knew.

Jason got up and walked down the hall. Passing the bathroom, he saw his mom in front of the mirror. He noticed the deep wrinkles in the space between her eyebrows. He'd seen that worried look before and was secretly glad that this time Brandy had put it there, not him.

His mother reached for the hairspray.

"Wait! Mom!" Jason yelled, running in and grabbing her hand.

Mrs. Richards shook her hand free. "Jason, please. Your dad and I are going to a Homeowners meeting to discuss Mr. Gammel and that satellite dish. I don't want to be late."

"I was going to remind you about the ozone. Every little *pssst* of hairspray, and another micro-layer disappears."

Looking perplexed, Mrs. Richards set her hairspray on the shelf. Satisfied, Jason hurried downstairs.

"Dad, will Mr. Horowitz be at the meeting?"

"Sure. I guess Paul will be there. All the neighbors are going."

"I want you to talk to him."

Mr. Richards gave his son a quizzical look. "What about?"

"I want you to tell him to quit putting chemicals on his grass. Before you know it, we'll be like the mastodons."

"Mastodons?"

"Yeah, Dad. We'll be extinct. It'll be the fault of people like Mr. Horowitz and Mom."

"Let me get this straight. Your mother is poisoning the atmosphere with Paul's chemicals."

"No! She's poisoning it with hairspray. Will you do it? Will you talk to Mr. Horowitz?"

Behind him, Jason could hear Brandy thumping down the steps.

"What's this? Mom and Mr. Horowitz? Get real, Jason! Pu-leeese."

"Mastodons," Mr. Richards answered in a tired voice.

"Oh, is that all. Then you ought to start with Jason.

Every time he comes in after being with Eddie, he's covered with gross red hairs. Both of them are. You can check the vacuum cleaner, if you don't believe me. Half the bag is filled with long red hairs. Talk about mastodons. If I didn't know better, I'd say he had one in the backyard that he was keeping a secret."

Jason froze. His heart pounded like crazy.

"Young lady," Mr. Richards said, ignoring Brandy's reference to Tiny. "Conservation obviously means a great deal to your brother. I would appreciate it if you would respect his feelings."

"Feelings!" Brandy shrieked. "What do *you* know about feelings? "

Mr. Richards raised his eyebrows. "Brandy, this boy, whoever he is, probably got busy."

"Flipping hamburgers? How busy can you get doing that?"

"If it's his job, he can be pretty busy."

Brandy made a noise that sounded like *harumph.* "Talking to every girl who comes in to order a chicken salad and a diet drink." She stopped and glared at Mr. Richards. "I hate you."

Dad looked surprised. "What did I do?"

"You're laughing. You don't understand. You won't let me go up to McDonald's with DeeDee." Brandy's sunburned nose was growing redder by the second. She was really turning on the tears.

"Brandy, your mother and I need you to stay home with Jason."

"Why is it always me who has to stay home with Jason?" Brandy sniffled. "I don't even get paid."

"You get an allowance."

"Hah. You call what you give me an allowance? Homeless people make more money."

Some things you just didn't say. Dad's face was almost as red as Brandy's nose. "That's enough of your smart talk, young lady," he bellowed. "Now go to your room."

Three minutes later, Jason's heart returned to normal. "Um, Dad, does that mean you'll talk to Mr. Horowitz?"

Mr. Richards looked puzzled until he recalled their earlier discussion. "I can't promise it will change anything. The agenda is Mr. Gammel's satellite dish, not lawn chemicals, but I'll see what I can do."

"Thanks, Dad."

Mrs. Richards came downstairs and laid her hand on Mr. Richards's arm. She gave Jason a wink before lifting his baseball cap and kissing him lightly on the forehead, enveloping him in the perfume he had bought her for Christmas. It was called Beautiful. She was.

Chapter 12

Jason's Decision

Jason was watching the car back out of the driveway when the phone rang.

"I got it!" Brandy yelled from her bedroom. Elvis was singing softer now, almost crooning.

Love me tender
Love me dear . . .

Jason smiled as he heard Brandy giggle once, twice, three times. He didn't have pick up the phone to know who was on the other end. The burger flipper was back in the picture and Brandy was in heaven.

Meanwhile, across the street, Mr. Horowitz's garage door rolled up. Dr. Dakos had already gone by in his Volvo. It was a regular caravan. If Jason watched long enough, he'd see most of their neighbors cruise down East Street.

It was scary.

By tomorrow night Gamma Rays's dish might be gone.

With Brandy occupied on the phone, Jason slipped out the back door. Minutes later, he was in the woods explaining everything to Eddie.

"We need to warn Gamma Rays."

"Why?"

"Because he's a nice guy. You should have heard him with his mother. And you don't take television programs away from people for no good reason." Jason knew about that firsthand. "Besides, it bugs me how my mom got sumo wrestlers on our TV the same as his mom."

"So? You and I watch the same programs lots of times."

"Not sumo wrestling or 'Howdy Doody.' If there's a connection between what's happening on his TV and ours, there might be a connection to Tiny. I know it sounds weird, but what if a bunch of TV signals got mixed up, and instead of going to Gamma Rays's television set, they got into ours?"

"Can't happen. Even if it could, TV signals aren't the same as a mastodon. I've stared at that stupid satellite, and I never saw one itsy-bitsy baby mastodon bounce out and go strolling down the sidewalk. It's impossible."

"I still have to go back over there."

"Suit yourself," Eddie said. "But don't expect me to

come running to your defense when the highly nutso and extremely dangerous Mr. Gamma Rays gets tired of you pestering him with a bunch of ridiculous questions about 'Howdy Doody,' sumo wrestlers, and a stupid satellite dish he has no business owning in the first place. Don't expect me to save you when he stuffs you in one of his miniature coffins just to shut you up."

"That does it!"

Eddie threw his hands in the air. "I'm kidding! I'm kidding!"

"I bet!"

"Jase, cool it! You'll do what you want to do. You know why? Because you're pigheaded, Jason Richards. For some people that might be a good thing, but for you it's not. You're liable to get yourself in a bunch of trouble. Me too. That's another thing. In addition to being pigheaded, you are the most selfish person I know."

Jason was shocked. He'd been called stubborn plenty of times, mostly by Brandy, which didn't count. But nobody had ever told Jason he was selfish.

"Why don't you think about me for a change?" Eddie continued. "What am I supposed to tell your mother if you don't come back? 'Excuse me, Mrs. Richards, I know this sounds strange, but your son might have been done in by some kook who watches "Howdy Doody." Oh, and by the way, don't stand too close to that satellite dish or you might get smacked in the head with a mastodon.' Jase, they're liable to lock me up. I don't know about you, but I don't want to spend the rest of my days in some hospital for the mentally deranged."

"Yeah, yesterday you were worried about going to jail, and before that it was being a mastodon's last meal."

"Somebody's got to think of these things."

"Well, I'm still going over to see Mr. Gammel."

"Fine, but if you don't come back in exactly thirty minutes, I'm calling the police. After that, I'm calling the dog warden to come get Tiny."

Chapter 13

Mr. Fix-it's Accident

Jason kept his hands shoved deep in his pockets as he headed down the block toward Gamma Rays's house. What the rest of the neighborhood did wasn't his fault. Or was it?

He felt bad for Gamma Rays. Nobody asked to be the maniac of the neighborhood. Nobody needed to be on the agenda of a secret meeting.

It's not fair, Jason thought. He needed to warn Gamma Rays. Besides if Tiny, Howdy Doody, and the sumo wrestlers somehow fit together and had anything to do with the satellite dish, then Jason had to know tonight. Tomorrow might be too late.

Gamma Rays answered the doorbell on the first ring.

"I didn't mean to toss you out this morning."

Gamma Rays was sitting at his desk while Jason inspected some of his souvenirs. "Mother's programs require fancy calculations and delicate fine tuning on that silver dish outside. One would think I could write a software program to handle the adjustments automatically." Gamma Rays chuckled. "My, how I love to tinker, and I do love a challenge."

Jason set the carving of a mountain lion back on the shelf. "My mother says you're a genius."

Gamma Rays blushed. "How perceptive of her. Now what were you saying earlier about your mastodon?"

Jason jumped. He never admitted to having a mastodon! Maybe Eddie was right and Gamma Rays couldn't be trusted. Jason should be careful.

"No, I, uh, was *asking* about mastodons because of something we studied in school." Jason's heart pounded in his chest. He didn't want to believe outrageous things about this seemingly nice man. Still, he had Tiny's safety to consider.

Gamma Rays put his head back and laughed. "Leaping electrodes, protons, and quarks! Calm down! I didn't mean you had a privately owned mastodon."

Jason sighed with relief as his heart returned to normal. Okay, Gamma Rays didn't know about Tiny. But just to be on the safe side, he'd go slow with what he revealed.

"I was wondering," Jason continued. "Could there be a leftover mastodon wandering around without anyone knowing? They wouldn't all have to be dead like dinosaurs, would they? In this movie I saw, a prehistoric man was found in a chunk of ice. When the people got him thawed out, he was still alive. So, could that happen to a mastodon?"

"Mmmm. Interesting speculation but I hardly think so. You see, in the past, mastodons have been discovered preserved much the way your mother keeps food in her freezer. But as the mastodon's body thawed, it decayed rather quickly. After all, the mastodon had died. The freezing temperatures only preserved the body. So to answer your question, Jason, nothing you've described has ever occurred. Not that I know of anyway."

"Nothing," Jason said urgently. "No living mastodons."

"Absolutely not." Gamma Rays shook his head. "Such an occurrence would be quite important. Ecology and natural history, which includes the study of mastodons, are particular interests of mine. My colleagues would have notified me immediately."

Concentrating, Gamma Rays rubbed his hand across his wide forehead and rested his elbows on his knees. "You see," he continued, "even if a herd of mastodons had survived the Great Ice Age, it could hardly survive in our world today. And it's hardly likely a mastodon herd could go completely undiscovered."

Jason leaned closer as Gamma Rays lowered his voice until it was barely above a whisper. "What I'm trying to say is, how does one go about hiding anything as colossal as a mastodon?"

"Yeah, I see what you mean."

Gamma Rays glanced at his watch. He shook his head sadly. "I don't mean to toss you out on your ear again, but there's a meeting tonight that has me more than a bit upset."

"You know about the meeting?" Jason swallowed. "I was going to warn you."

Gamma Rays didn't hear. "If only your mother had gotten 'Howdy Doody' instead . . ." Gamma Rays's voice drifted off.

Jason frowned. "Howdy Doody?"

"Your mother seemed worried about your father. Something about a storm and how she didn't want him crawling around on the roof fiddling with your TV antenna. She suspected my satellite dish was playing havoc with your television. What could I do? I offered to improve your TV reception with a special receiver."

Gamma Rays smiled. "I didn't tell her I planned to use my bothersome satellite dish to beam a stronger signal into your set. Simple procedure! I upgraded the feed horn on the dish and hooked a receiver to your TV. That's what that little black box on top of your VCR is. But then your mother got my mother's sumo wrestlers by mistake. Catastrophic!" Gamma Rays exclaimed.

"But how . . . "

Gamma Rays's eyes flashed. "Don't interrupt. I'm not finished. I attend auctions. A couple of months ago, I went to an auction of surplus government electronic parts and bought a box of tubes and resisters. Fantastic find! There, buried in a tiny plastic case, were two peculiar diodes that looked like they belonged in a remote control. Mother was unhappy because she couldn't get her stations fast enough. What could it hurt? I put a diode in her remote and . . . zappo."

Zappo?

"The next thing I knew, it was 'Howdy Doody' time. Mother does love Howdy Doody. I still had the other diode," Gamma Rays continued. "I thought if your mother got Howdy instead of those nasty sumo wrestlers, perhaps she could squelch the neighborhood protest. The diode fit perfectly under the memory button on your remote."

Jason was beginning to feel lightheaded. He'd pushed the memory button right before Tiny appeared in their living room.

Jason opened his mouth, but nothing came out. The most important question was waiting to be asked, and there he stood, completely speechless.

Chapter 14

Through Space and Time

A two-part riddle was keeping Jason awake. What did a fifties program like "Howdy Doody" and a baby mastodon have in common? That was the first part of the riddle. The second part was more difficult. How *exactly* did Tiny get here? He had to know that to figure out a way to get him back.

Jason twisted and turned in his sheets. He socked his pillow, trying to make a comfortable dent. Finally, sometime before dawn, Jason called Eddie on the cordless phone from his bed.

"Nah, that's too far out," Eddie whispered on the other end. "Things like that don't happen."

"It did happen," Jason whispered back.

Eddie listened carefully as Jason repeated what he'd said the first time.

"We already know Gamma Rays used his satellite

dish to beam sumo wrestlers into our TV."

"Jase, there is a big difference between sumo wrestlers who stay inside a television set and a live mastodon that pops into your living room. What you're talking about is science fiction."

"Except Tiny is real."

"Excuse me for forgetting."

Jason had to work at keeping his voice low. It was hot and stuffy under the sheets, but he couldn't risk his parents hearing him. "I told you what Gamma Rays said about adjusting his satellite dish for 'Howdy Doody' time. Don't you get it, Eddie? Not 'Howdy Doody' reruns. 'Howdy Doody' *time*. Gamma Rays is fooling around with time."

"Right. Using his zapper." Eddie paused. "Hey, Jase, you sure you're not talking in your sleep?"

"So whatever Gamma Rays did to get 'Howdy Doody' live from the fifties must be the same thing that got us Tiny live from the Ice Age," Jason went on. "It's got to be the zapper. When Gamma Rays stuck that diode thing inside, he made that little electronic gadget so powerful. You saw me, Eddie. All I did was point it . . ." Jason's voice drifted off.

"That's it!" Jason almost shouted. "Gamma Rays's satellite dish! Before I pressed the red memory button, I pointed the remote at Gamma Rays's satellite dish! Talk about power! From inside the house, through brick walls, and everything! After that, I pointed it at the TV set and pressed the red button again."

Eddie was silent as what Jason told him sunk in. "Wow," he said at last. "If what you're saying is true, imagine what would happen if the wrong people found out."

"Don't you ever listen? That's what I've been saying all along. Think what would happen to Tiny. We've got to make Gamma Rays send Tiny back to where he came from."

Eddie was incredulous. "I thought we weren't supposed to tell anyone. Now you're going to trust Gamma Rays with Tiny?" Eddie's voice started to squeak. "If Gamma Rays is zapping mastodons into people's houses, what's to stop him from zapping you? Geez, Jase! You could wind up on Pluto or Mars."

"It's time, not place. Besides, Gamma Rays wouldn't do that."

"Maybe not on purpose. Maybe it could be an accident. What difference does it make? You could wind up on the moon way before Neil Armstrong could bring you back!"

Gulp. "That's why you have to go with me," Jason said.

"Me? No way. I'm not going to be around when you point that zapper. I'm too young to die."

"What about Tiny?"

"Tiny's an animal. I'm human," Eddie said. "That's got to count for something."

"But Tiny needs us."

"So does my mother."

"I don't know what that has to do with Tiny," Jason said softly.

"Do me a favor. When you go back to sleep, dream on it."

"I will, Eddie. I promise. But who else is there?"

"Except me. Yeah, Jase. Right."

Jason was careful not to make any noise as he crept through the kitchen that morning. From his bedroom window, he'd watched his parents leave the house and drive down the block toward work.

Jason grabbed a couple of cereal boxes from the cabinet, a milk carton from the refrigerator, and two spoons from a kitchen drawer. His parents were gone, so it was safe to do what he and Eddie had planned for Tiny.

Balancing the cereal and milk in his arms, Jason rushed to where Eddie was already waiting. Above him, Brandy's stereo snapped on, loud and blaring. In spite of himself, Jason had to laugh.

Deep in my heart there's a trembling question.
Still I am sure that the answer is going
to come somehow.

He'd escaped just in time.

A few minutes later, he and Eddie were sitting on a log, eating their breakfast out of boxes.

"Look, I've been thinking," Eddie said. "Maybe

Gamma Rays wouldn't do anything stupid, but you never know. Maybe I ought to go with you just in case."

Jason breathed a sigh of relief. "We can't leave Tiny alone in the woods. Not in the daytime," he said. "Do you think he'll be OK in the garage?"

"What about your bossy sister?"

"She's upstairs listening to Elvis. She wouldn't come down the steps unless Elvis himself rang the doorbell."

Eddie slurped another spoonful of cereal. "Bet you never thought how you're going to get Tiny from here to your garage."

Jason grinned. "We're going to cover him with my bedspread."

Cornflakes blew out of Eddie's mouth. He started to choke.

"Bedspread!" he said, picking soggy brown flakes off his shirt with his fingers. "You're going to walk a bedspread the size of an elephant out of the woods, through your backyard, around the side of your house, up your driveway, and into your garage? And then, after we talk to Gamma Rays, we're going to walk a bedspread back down the driveway, around the house, through the yard, and back into the woods all over again? Are you crazy?"

"You got a better idea?"

Eddie fell silent. "No."

Jason glanced at Tiny, who, unaware of the panic he was causing, was observing a mother robin teaching her young to fly. Tiny had been with them for four days now. Jason bet Tiny missed his mother a lot.

"Let's go," Jason said.

Except for Tiny's trunk, which he kept poking outside the bedspread, and his tail, which he carried straight up like a TV antenna, the covering worked perfectly. As long as the boys could keep Tiny's trunk inside, they wouldn't worry about his tail. After all, if anyone saw them walking Jason's bedspread through the yard, the last thing in the world, they'd suspect was a mastodon. So, with Jason holding the clothesline fastened around Tiny's neck, the three of them paraded through the opening in the woods and toward the Richards's garage.

Once inside, Jason pressed the button and the garage door whirred shut. He tossed the bedspread into a corner. "We'll be right back, fella."

"You better hope Brandy stays upstairs," Eddie said. "One squeal from our little friend and she'll come down real quick."

Jason took a deep breath and let it out again. "Stop worrying," he said. "You're making me nervous."

Chapter 15

Gamma

Gamma Rays was at his computer when Jason and Eddie pressed their foreheads against the glass doors.

Slowly Gamma Rays pushed himself up from his desk, walked toward the doors, and slid one open. "Ah, fission and fusion, you've multiplied!"

"Yeah, this is my best friend, Eddie," Jason replied quickly.

Suddenly Jason felt unsure. Judging from the photographs, Gamma Rays liked animals. He *seemed* nice. But what if Jason was wrong? What if Gamma Rays wanted to make a fast buck off a defenseless baby mastodon?

Jason started to tremble. The room was darker than he remembered. Okay, so yesterday the afternoon sun had streamed through the sliding glass doors. Now it was morning, and the sun hadn't come around to this part of the house yet.

Jason struggled to swallow. "Uh, what we came to tell you, sir, is that we have this little problem."

"Growing's more like it," Eddie interrupted.

"Right. A *growing* problem. If you don't help us, it'll be a regular disaster."

The inventor frowned. He sat down at his desk, clearly prepared for the worst. "Maybe you boys better fill me in."

The only time Jason paused was to take a breath. He didn't stop explaining until he was finished.

"*Megafauna* from the late Pleistocene! Phenomenal! Ah, yes. I suspected something like that could happen."

Jason's mouth dropped open in shock. "You thought it might?"

"My boy!" Unable to sit still any longer, Gamma Rays began pacing the room. "Everytime you cross two wires, you open possibilities never before dreamed possible." He stopped long enough to sweep the horizons with his hand. "And possibilities, like the mind, are endless."

Jason glanced nervously at Eddie, who responded by rolling his eyes. "Tell Eddie about the zapper," he said breathlessly. "He doesn't believe what you did."

"Ah, yes. There is that difficulty in comprehension. You see, I did it for Mother. She lives for her sports programs. Granted, we could use the cable sports network, but that doesn't light a candle to the satellite. And now," Gamma Rays grumbled, "our thoughtless neighbors demand that I remove my satellite dish."

Jason had been right! There *was* a connection!

"I thought maybe it was because you put that leftover government diode in *our* remote," Jason said cautiously. "I thought maybe that's how Tiny got zapped into our living room." He swallowed. "Has something like this happened before?"

Gamma Rays's face turned red. "To be truthful, when Howdy Doody appeared out of nowhere, I found myself toying with the idea. A little time travel might amuse Mother. What could it hurt, I figured, as long as it was only old TV signals I was picking up and they weren't going anywhere except to my television set. It never occurred to me that something like a mastodon might crash through the next dimension." Gamma Rays smiled broadly. "Imagine, a mastodon. A baby, you say?"

Jason nodded. "We can't take care of him any longer, but we don't want anything bad to happen to him. If we could just get him back where he came from, back to his mother in the Pleistocene."

Gamma Rays massaged his forehead. "Hmmmm. As much as I love a challenge, what we have here is a significant dilemma." Gamma Rays paused briefly.

"Gentlemen, have you heard about the theory of relativity: Every object in the universe has a gravitational field. The more massive the object is, the stronger its gravitational pull."

Gamma Rays rocked on his heels. "What this means

is that transporting a five-hundred-pound mastodon back to the Pleistocene is harder than floating a hippopotamus down White River Canyon in a canoe. None of my colleagues has been successful in transporting objects faster than the speed of light. I suspect what's happened is more along the line of particle physics, which is a bit more advanced than ordinary space travel. Are you with me?"

Jason and Eddie exchanged glances as Gamma Rays resumed pacing. "What happens is that particles break apart as they travel through space and time. You can imagine how important avoiding that problem would be." Gamma Rays paused to take a breath. "Such a discovery could revolutionize the world. Nothing would ever be the same."

"Why?"

"Think of it!" Gamma Rays exclaimed. "Instant transportation."

"Wow," Eddie interrupted. "We'd be rich."

Mr. Gammel sat down at his desk. He looked from Jason to Eddie then back to Jason. "Rich indeed!"

It was all Eddie needed. He was grinning so wide Jason expected his face to crack. Jason knew the look. Eddie was buying that zooming red sports car. The license plate would say IMRICH.

Meanwhile, Gamma Rays sat down in his chair and stared off into space. "Universities named in my honor! Stockbrokers lunching at the World Gammel Towers. Of course, I'd pose for statues."

Jason's shoulders slumped. What was the use? He should have known everyone would put money ahead of Tiny.

Jason gazed out the window at the exact place where the two panes crossed. If he concentrated hard enough, maybe he wouldn't bawl like a baby.

"You pose an interesting dilemma, my boy." Gamma Rays's hand squeezed Jason's shoulder. "Do we seek fame and fortune or do we set your beloved pet free and return him to his mother?" Gamma Rays stopped to clear his throat. "Alas, the pain of separation, animal or human, from its mother."

"Could you do it?" Jason was almost afraid to ask. "I mean, would you?"

"It is a challenge. Mmmm," he said, closing his eyes briefly. "I do love a challenge." Gamma Rays looked from one boy to the other. "Have either of you ever had a pet before? A dog, cat, monkey, crayfish?"

"Jason hasn't," Eddie answered.

"Well, then. The affection he holds for this mastodon is quite obvious."

Slowly Gamma Rays stood up and stretched. He walked around his desk, then sat back down in front of his computer.

"I'll be happy to try," he said, rubbing his finger thoughtfully against his lip. "Of course, it would be a very precise operation, and I'll need to meet your mastodon before we begin. I must know his exact size and weight."

Click, click. With a few strokes at the computer keyboard, a constellation appeared on the screen. *Click, click.* Gamma Rays tapped in the date, hit ENTER, and the screen changed.

"Behold tonight's universe!" Gamma Rays exclaimed, hitting a button. "Not as *we* see the sky, because the starlight we observe may have taken anywhere from eight to eight million years or longer to reach us here on earth. Just think, with the blink of an eye you are looking eight million years into the past! The stars we enjoy may not even exist anymore. But here, through the magic of science, technology, and pure projection, my computer screen reflects the true and present location of our galaxies!"

Gamma Rays hit another button. A calendar popped up. The boys watched, spellbound, as Gamma Rays's finger traced a line on the screen.

"Now according to this chart . . ." The scientist raised his eyebrows and smiled. "It's up to you. We could send Tiny back tomorrow. If we don't, we'd have to wait until December 23, 2026. Otherwise, with the constant shifting of the planets in our solar system, not to mention the other galaxies, we'd never get your mastodon through to the Pleistocene. Not in one piece, anyway."

"Not in one piece?" Jason exclaimed.

"Two thousand twenty-six? Excuse me." Eddie's face was full of doubt. "But how do you know all of this?"

Gamma Rays stiffened. "You boys want credentials?"

He reached behind him to the bookcase and pulled a thick book titled *Mysteries of the Universe* off the shelf. Jason noticed it had his name on it: Anthony P. Gammel. Waving his arm, Gamma Rays indicated the many plaques and certificates framed and hanging on the wall. Jason had seen them yesterday. Some were signed by famous presidents Jason had learned about in history class. Finally Gamma Rays opened his desk drawer and grabbed a handful of gold medals with bright-colored ribbons, which he dropped under Eddie's nose.

"And the software I'm using is from Mission Control in Houston. Of course, I've had to modify the program. I made my own CD-ROM. Technology, like everything else, changes overnight." Gamma Rays sighed. "I never thought I'd have to explain myself to two young rascals. Now, do you boys think you can get it together by tomorrow?"

Satisfied with his calculations, Gamma Rays turned the computer off.

Two seconds later, Jason heard a scream. It was a loud scream Jason would recognize anywhere.

Brandy!

Chapter 16

Brandy

"JASON!"

Jason and Eddie bolted for the patio door at the same time. Gamma Rays wasn't far behind.

"She must have found Tiny! Quick, you two go behind the garage," Jason shouted. "I'll take care of Brandy!"

"JA-A-A-A-SON!"

Brandy was standing—fists clenched, legs spread wide apart— barefoot in the middle of their driveway. She had a look that had "KILL" written all over it. Even from where Jason crouched in the bushes, he could feel the fire in Brandy's eyes.

She was really steamed. Not finding what or who she was looking for, she raised her head, shut her eyes, and screamed Jason's name again.

"JA-A-A-A-SON SCOTT RICH-AAAARRRDDDS!"

Brandy never saw Jason sneak up beside her in the driveway.

"You looking for me?" Jason said it so quietly Brandy nearly flew out of her skin. Jason smiled. He loved doing that to Brandy. He liked to think he was paying her back for squealing to Dad about watching television. The crack about "General Hospital" was *not* funny.

Hands on hips, Brandy glared at Jason. She thrust her head forward and jutted out her chin.

"OK," Brandy started, loud enough for the whole world to hear. "You're responsible. You and your goofball friend, Eddie. I know you are and don't say you're not."

Uh-oh. She'd been in the garage all right.

Jason stepped back. His arms fell limply to his sides.

"And you can wipe that startled, *'Who me?'* look off your face. It might work for Mom, but you can't fool me. The electricity is out again and it's all your fault."

Jason's heart pounded in his ears. Brandy *hadn't* found Tiny. What a relief!

Then Jason had a terrible thought. What if the electricity went out tomorrow?

Finding Brandy in the driveway gave Jason an idea. Someone had to help them with the problem of electricity, and Brandy was perfect for the job. Now if he could only convince her—without spilling the beans about Tiny.

Of course, Jason knew Brandy would never do

anything for him. And he couldn't pay her—he didn't have any money. In fact, he couldn't offer her anything she would want.

Jason stopped. There was *one* thing.

Jason started slowly, trying to sound casual, as though he was about to say the most natural thing in the world.

"Hey, um, what if I told you I knew a way for you to meet Elvis?"

Recovered from her tantrum, Brandy gave Jason her usual weirdo look. "Give me a break."

"No, really." Jason tried again, this time raising his eyebrow slightly. "What if I told you I knew a way for you to meet Elvis?"

He could see the wheels turning as she started to look at him a little differently. Brandy's eyes narrowed even more. Hands folded across her chest, she leaned forward. "Elvis Presley? The *real* Elvis Presley?"

Jason nodded. "Eddie and I have been working on this science project."

"Hey." Brandy straightened. "I don't get straight *A*'s for nothing. I already know what it is."

"You do?" Jason's heart stopped. What a jerk he'd been to think he could keep a secret from Brandy.

"First the lettuce. Then the grass clippings and manure. All those red hairs. Anybody could figure it out. All those camera men and reporters running around probably know too. They're just waiting until the exact moment to pounce. Some secret discovery.

111

You'll do all the work and then the government will step in."

Jason felt his heart crash to his knees.

"So if you think you're going to get all the credit for inventing the world's biggest, reddest tomato with this super-duper fertilizer you guys are making in the backyard, well, just give it up."

"What?" Jason could hardly believe his ears.

"Ha!" Brandy shrieked, thinking she'd uncovered Jason's secret. "See, I was right!"

Jason bit his lip just in time. For a moment, he'd almost denied it. What a mistake that would have been.

"OK," he said, letting Brandy think she was right. "But I still know how you can meet Elvis, the real you-ain't-nothin'-but-a-hound-dog Elvis. You can either help me out or you can forget the whole thing. I'm only going to give you one chance. If you blow it, you might *never* get to see Elvis."

"Honestly, Jason. You don't think I believe those stories in the tabloids, do you? Elvis Presley is dead."

"Maybe," Jason said, raising his eyebrows. "Maybe not. What if I also said I had a legitimate reason for you to go up to McDonald's? That *is* where your new boyfriend works, isn't it? And I wouldn't even tell Mom or Dad."

Brandy cocked her head and stared. "You're kidding."

"No."

"What do I have to do?"

When she said that, Jason knew he had her. He started to explain. "It's all electrical."

"I knew it!" Brandy slammed one fist into the palm of her other hand so hard Jason jumped. "I knew you were responsible for the blackouts! I knew it all along!"

"No!" Jason shouted. They were running out of time. If he couldn't get Brandy to help, he'd have to find someone else.

"It's not me. But if anything happens when I do the next part of my experiment tomorrow, then it's all ruined. I need you to watch the construction crews on Maple Avenue—the ones working on those new buildings Mom and Dad are always complaining about. You can see them from McDonald's. When the work crews stop for lunch, I need you to call me on the phone. There can't be a break in power during the next stage. It's crucial."

"Crucial?" Brandy crossed her arms and stared. Her nose wrinkled a thousand different ways. She cleared her throat and blushed. "Um," she stammered, obviously embarrassed by having to ask her younger brother anything. "You know what you said about Elvis? Are you serious? Because if you are, it better be Elvis the King. I don't want some cheap imitation."

Jason nodded. "I am. Blue suede shoes and all. There's only one other thing."

"I knew it."

"You can't tell anyone. Not anyone."

When Jason stuck out his hand, they shook.

That was when Brandy looked down, discovered she was wearing her teddy bear pajamas, and ran shrieking into the house.

"Yeeee-aaaaauggghhhhhhh!"

Jason stood in the middle of the driveway and scratched his head. Now he'd have to hope that desperately in love Brandy would remember what she was supposed to do once she got to McDonald's. He would have to pray that totally witless Brandy didn't become so involved watching her burger-flipping boyfriend stuff french fries in paper sacks that she forgot her mission. He had to know for sure when the construction crews took their lunch break. He had to know for sure that Gamma Rays would have uninterrupted power for Tiny's journey back to the Pleistocene.

What a terrifying thought.

Tiny's life depended on Brandy.

Chapter 17

Brandy's
Secret Date

Jason was brushing Tiny's red fur with long, loving strokes. He liked the way it looked, smooth and shiny. When the sun shone through the clearing, the slanted rays turned Tiny's coat to spun copper. He had never seen anything so beautiful.

"It's our last night." Jason's voice caught in his throat. He hoped Eddie hadn't noticed. "We ought to spend it with Tiny."

Eddie glanced up from the magazine he was reading. "Our folks will say no."

"Not if they think we're camping in the backyard."

Jason sat down beside Eddie and pulled a flashlight out of his knapsack. "If they look out the window, they'll see the tent." Jason tossed the flashlight in his hand. "They just won't see us *in* the tent. Get it?" Jason flicked the flashlight on and then off again.

"What if your mom gets up in the middle of the night and comes out to check on us? She might want to be sure the boogey man didn't get us. I bet you never thought of that."

"Yeah, I did."

"So?"

"Snakes."

"Snakes?" Eddie yelped.

Tiny stopped eating. With his high forehead and eyes wide-open, Jason thought Tiny looked awfully wise. He wondered if Tiny knew about snakes.

"My mom's afraid of snakes," Jason said. He held the flashlight under his chin, snapping it on so it gave him an eerie appearance. "She'd have to use a flashlight if she wanted to check on us, but we have the flashlight." Jason clicked the flashlight off for emphasis.

"You only have one flashlight in your house?" Eddie wasn't so sure.

"No. We have two, but trust me." Jason smiled. "Before the evening's over, we'll have both flashlights. In the morning, I'll make sure my mother knows we survived the night."

The boys waited until Tiny was taking his afternoon nap before pitching the tent in Jason's backyard. Then they went back to taking care of Tiny.

In some ways, it seemed to Jason that the day was endless. In other ways, it seemed to pass too quickly. There wasn't enough time to play with Tiny. Nerfball.

Frisbee. Hide-and-seek was best. When Tiny hid his head behind a tree, he thought the rest of his body was hidden too. Jason and Eddie couldn't stop laughing. For that bit of time, there was no tomorrow. There was no dangerous trip ahead for Tiny. There was no saying good-bye. But all too soon, the shadows lengthened, then disappeared as the sky turned from gray to purple to black velvet with more stars than Jason could ever hope to count.

"Are you boys comfortable?" Mrs. Richards poked her head inside the tent where both boys were lying on their stomachs.

"Mom, we're camping out. We're not supposed to be comfortable."

"Oh, yes, I know. I just meant . . . never mind. I'll leave the back-porch light on. The door is open if you boys decide to trade the hard ground for a nice soft bed."

"We won't change our minds, Mom."

"Now?" Eddie whispered as Mrs. Richards headed back toward the house.

"Not yet. We've got to wait for my dad."

"Your dad?" Eddie griped as Jason turned the flashlight off and hid it under his pillow. "What is this, a family reunion?"

Jason took a swig of cola. "Hey, can I help it if they love me?"

Fortunately they didn't have to wait long.

"I thought you boys might need this." Mr. Richards handed Jason a flashlight.

"Gee, Mr. Richards," Eddie said. "You don't know how much better I feel having this flashlight."

Jason waited as his father checked the poles before heading back toward the house.

"Now?" Eddie asked when the screen door slapped shut.

"Not yet."

"Not yet? Now what?"

Two headlights appeared in the driveway. A car door slammed. Not very loud. It was a sneaky kind of slam that made Jason's ears perk right up. Jason could hear the tingly sound of Brandy's voice and the sound of footsteps in the driveway. They were coming around to the back door.

Somebody was with Brandy, but it wasn't a girl. Jason knew because Brandy wasn't making her usual shrieking noise. Oddly enough, she wasn't giggling like a hyena either.

Jason raised up on his elbows. He grabbed his binoculars. This was serious stuff.

Here at last was French Fry Freddie in the flesh. But wasn't Brandy supposed to be with Karen?

Jason frowned. Brandy was heading up the steps to the back porch with her boyfriend close behind. Now they were standing under the light. Brandy only came up to his shoulder.

Eddie was also staring through another set of binoculars. "Look at them," Eddie hissed. "Kissing!"

Startled, Brandy stopped. She peered out into the darkness.

"What was that?" Brandy whispered.

Freddie tried to grab Brandy's shoulders, but she'd stepped out from under the porch light so she could see.

"There in the yard." Brandy pointed directly at them. "It's my brother, the measly toad, and one of his worthless friends."

"Oh, Brandy, Brandy, my darling, Brandy," Eddie moaned. He put his arm to his mouth and made loud kissing noises. "One more slobby, blobbery kiss."

Jason started to giggle. He was trying to look through the binoculars, but he was laughing so hard the binoculars kept knocking into his nose.

"Jason!"

Jason had never heard Brandy scream quietly before. She had to. If their parents heard, Brandy would be dog meat. Meanwhile Brandy's boyfriend had hopped in his car and made a speedy exit.

Jason crawled slowly out of the tent. Careful, he reminded himself. Already he was wishing he and Eddie hadn't been so stupid. If Brandy got mad, she wouldn't help them tomorrow. They needed Brandy. Tiny needed Brandy.

When Jason got close enough to where Brandy could see him, he let his shoulders slump and stared at his toes. It was supposed to make him look pitiful. He'd never admit it to Brandy, but he'd learned a lot from having an older sister.

"Yes?" Jason said sheepishly.

Brandy was tapping her foot. He had to assume her hands were on her hips, her eyes narrowed into slits.

"Don't you creeps have anything better to do?"

Jason picked at his fingernail. "We were just having a little fun. Besides, we didn't know it was you. Not at first."

"Get real."

Gradually Jason raised his head. At the same time, he widened his eyes with what he hoped was a look of pure innocence. "I thought you went to the mall with Karen. That's what you said at dinner. How was I supposed to know you'd come home with a boy? You were in the car with him and everything. You're not supposed to."

That caught Brandy off guard. "I-I-I was with Karen, until she got sick. You won't tell?" she said in a rush. "Mom and Dad would never believe me. You know they think I'm still a baby."

Jason crossed his heart and held up his hand in a solemn promise. If Brandy expected Jason to keep his promise, she'd better remember to keep hers and watch the construction crews from McDonald's tomorrow—or else.

Jason waited until Brandy shut the door before heading back toward the tent. Except for the lights on the porch and in the kitchen, the house was dark. Jason ducked his head inside the tent. He fastened the front tent flaps securely behind him.

"Now?" Eddie whispered. He had the sleeping bags rolled up and ready to go.

"Yeah. Now."

Slowly the boys crawled out the back, dragging their sleeping bags behind them. They didn't dare stand up until they reached the woods. They didn't make a sound until they reached the clearing.

There were some times when Jason couldn't laugh, not even at Eddie. This was one of those times. He and Eddie were in their sleeping bags, and Eddie was making frog noises, probably because Brandy had called Jason a measly toad. Jason couldn't respond. There was too much to think and worry about.

"It doesn't seem right," Jason said after a while. "When we finally get Tiny trained . . . " His voice broke. "That's when we have to get rid of him." Jason rolled over on his side so he could see Eddie as he talked. Behind him, Tiny was curled up in a red fuzzy ball and snoring lightly. Jason was careful to keep his voice low. "He knows his name and everything."

Eddie agreed. "Did you notice how he goes to the same place now to poop? That's important, Jase. The guy definitely has class."

"And he's quiet waiting for us because he knows we'll come back. Sometimes in the morning, he's already awake when I get here. Did I tell you that?"

"Only a thousand times, but you know what? We still can't keep him."

Jason didn't need Eddie to point out the facts. "Tiny will be better off with his mother. We're doing the best thing." Jason wiped his eyes on his sleeve. "I mean, we're doing the *only* thing," he said.

"Not exactly," Eddie said after a long and awkward silence. "We could still try to find a *better* place for Tiny than with us, like maybe with some nice scientists. What if Gamma Rays screws up? You think it was a safe place where Tiny came from, but it wasn't. What if instead of landing on the peaceful frozen tundra with a bunch of other mastodons, Tiny winds up in the middle of a fight between two saber-tooth tigers? What if he ends up in a pit surrounded by a bunch of Cro-Magnons with an arsenal of poison-tipped spears? What if Tiny's trusty friends screw up? What then, Jason? How are you going to feel about that?"

Jason gulped. "I don't know."

Just then Jason heard something. "Shhh!"

Jason scrambled out of his sleeping bag and hurried over to Tiny, who was rolling about and making strange yelping sounds in his sleep. Jason began stroking his mastodon and talking to him in a soft voice. He didn't want his little friend to worry. After all, he was just a little baby with a long trip ahead of him.

Chapter 18

If You Say Good-bye

At ten o'clock the next morning, Jason and Eddie stared out from the clearing.

Mrs. Huddleston and a bunch of other ladies were parading up and down the sidewalk pushing baby strollers and waving homemade signs. Just then two TV vans pulled up to the curb.

Jason sighed heavily. "What rotten luck. It must be their last effort before tonight's hearing."

Beside him, Eddie whispered. "Maybe we ought to reconsider and send Tiny back in the year 2026. Of course by then, instead of reading books, you'll probably be writing them. *One Hundred and One Ways to Hide a Hungry Mastodon.* Only it'll never make the bestseller list because . . . guess what? We'll still be keeping Tiny a secret."

"Cute, Eddie. Get the bedspread."

A few minutes later, Tiny was shifting his weight from side to side, swinging his trunk, and holding his precious T-shirt. As much as Jason tried, the bedspread wouldn't stay put.

"Tiny, calm down!" Jason didn't mean to sound impatient. Feeling badly, he petted the mastodon's head. Tiny was just a baby, and he was only picking up on their own nervousness. Tiny knew something was going on. He just didn't understand what.

But there couldn't be any delays. The calculations for Tiny's time travel left no margin for error.

Jason pulled the bedspread lower in the front while Eddie straightened it in the back. Then, as Jason held the clothesline tightly in his hand, the three of them stepped out of the woods, just as they had the day before. This time, though, Eddie stared skyward, whistling nonchalantly as he strolled along beside the mastodon. Jason, meanwhile, kept his face fixed straight ahead. With legs like rubber, he led Tiny toward Gamma Rays's basement.

As soon as they were close enough, Gamma Rays slid the glass doors open and whisked them inside. "Whew! Those reporters had me worried. I kept rotating the satellite dish as a distraction."

Gamma Rays clasped his hands as Jason let the spread drop to the floor. "Everything's going to be OK, fella," Jason said, hugging his pet. "Mr. Gammel's going to help you get back to your mother."

Tiny trumpeted softly. He pressed his furry head against Jason's chest.

But even as he said it, Jason wasn't sure. Gamma Rays might be a genius, but what they were about to do was pretty scary stuff. Zapping Tiny into the right time period was tricky enough, but could Gamma Rays get Tiny back to his mother? Jason closed his eyes and shuddered as everything Eddie said last night came back to haunt him.

"I trust you boys have taken care of the matter of electricity," Gamma Rays said. "Or rather, the possibility of a lack of it. According to all calculations, and I've done each a minimum of a dozen times, it will take fifty-eight minutes, thirty-three seconds to zap Tiny back to the Pleistocene. One fraction of a second, one therm less power than calculated, is all it takes to put your little friend in a hostile environment. Perish the thought!"

"Yes, sir," Jason answered quickly, desperately hoping Brandy didn't go all googly-eyed over French Fry Freddie and forget what she was supposed to do at McDonald's. "My sister has your phone number. She'll call when the construction crews stop for lunch and again when they go back to work."

Gamma Rays swiveled around in his chair. He leaned forward across his desk and pressed the row of buttons next to the terminal.

Jason had never seen Gamma Rays concentrate so hard. Even so, he crossed his fingers and hoped he'd made the right decision.

OK, so Gamma Rays wasn't exactly trained to send mastodons hurtling through space. It wasn't anything like his old job with *National Geographic,* but what about all the books he'd read? What about the stuff he wrote and the awards he got? Didn't that prove the man was a genius? After all, who else but a genius would experiment with time travel?

Eddie nudged Jason and nodded toward Gamma Rays. Look at him, Jason thought, peering at that computer screen for all it was worth. Jason bit his lip and prayed. Besides, who else was there except Gamma Rays?

Completely absorbed with what he was doing, Gamma Rays rotated his satellite dish electronically into the proper position. It was a quarter to twelve.

Jason brushed the ring of soft fur around Tiny's neck while Eddie rubbed behind Tiny's ear. It was hard to believe that only a week ago, he and Eddie had been in the living room fighting over the remote. And now here they were, saying good-bye.

Chapter 19

Zappo!

No one said a word. Not Jason. Not Eddie. Not Gamma Rays. Instead they listened to the ticking of the clock and stared at the phone. If eyes could melt plastic, Jason thought, the phone would have turned into a bubbling mass minutes ago.

Why didn't Brandy call?

There could only be one reason. She had forgotten why Jason had sent her to McDonald's. Instead of observing the construction crews, she was giggling with her burger-flipping boyfriend.

How could Jason have been foolish enough to trust Brandy?

Jason tried to shake the dark thoughts from his head. His eyes stung with fear and apprehension. He had to think positively. His sister had never let him down before. Would she now?

Who else could he have asked other than Brandy? The only other person was Eddie, but he needed Eddie to help with Tiny. He also needed moral support. No, Jason thought. He'd made the right decision with Brandy.

Now the only thing that stood between Tiny and Tiny's mother was fifty-eight minutes of uninterrupted electricity, 10,000 years, and who knows how many miles of time travel back to the Pleistocene.

Jason shivered, remembering Gamma Rays's explanation of his last untested theory.

Gamma Rays had been twirling the knobs on an auxiliary box to the right of the computer terminal when, without warning, he'd stopped and cocked his head.

"Racing electrons!" he said suddenly. "That was my inspiration! Back in the seventies, I wrote an article about the space program. Scientists at the Fermi National Accelerator Laboratory were racing massive electrons, two thousand times their normal amount. Of course, the only way they could do this was by strengthening the magnetic field. So they constructed a ring of magnets. Imagine . . . I suppose smart boys like yourselves know about magnets," he said. "What you might not understand are the magnetic fields existing between people."

When Jason frowned, the scientist jabbed his finger in the air. "A mother loves her child. Correct? A child loves its mother."

"Yeah."

"Good." Gamma Rays continued. "You see, until the child reaches a certain stage, separation between the two is intolerable because the magnetic pull is at its peak. But is this pull measurable? We measure everything else in this world—calories, intelligence—but can we measure love? And if so, what—*who*—would it serve?" He paused to flip a wall switch. "I think we have the answer here."

The light Jason felt was warm and bright. When Gamma Rays beamed the light on Tiny, the baby mastodon blinked and shook his head in approval.

"Now I want everyone standing ten feet apart," Gamma Rays said in a no-nonsense kind of voice. "Jason, you stand here on this line. Leave your mastodon friend there."

Jason went to where Gamma Rays pointed without hesitation. Tiny, on the other hand, extended his trunk, making the distance less than ten feet.

Gamma Rays turned to Eddie. "Move him back, son. These calculations must be quite precise."

Gamma Rays set a black metal box on the floor. When he flashed the light on the box, it began to whine, growing higher and higher in pitch. Suddenly the box fell silent, and the computer began printing at breakneck speed.

"Wheee-oooo! I love a challenge!"

Gamma Rays held the printouts to his nose. "Just as I suspected! The magnetic field between this mastodon calf and his mother has been weakened."

"Weakened!" Jason almost shouted. "How?"

"You," the scientist accused.

"Me? What'd I do?"

"Not you alone. Both of you. By allowing this mastodon to become your pet, he substituted you as his mother. That's not necessarily bad," Gamma Rays added, softening his voice. "Otherwise, this little calf might have died of loneliness and starvation. Still, in order to get him back, that magnetic pull must be as tight as a rubber band. Attention now!" Gamma Rays addressed Eddie. "Turn Tiny slightly to the west so I can take another reading."

This time, Tiny stood almost perfectly still. Only his small ears moved. Jason was amazed. For a baby, Tiny was behaving extraordinarily well under very difficult circumstances. Could he possibly understand what they were trying to accomplish?

Gamma Rays scratched his chin and looked directly at Jason. "I'm satisfied. Now your sister will have to provide the final insurance, which, I'm sad to say, is not much. These theories, after all, are untested. You both understand that?"

Jason and Eddie nodded. "Yes."

When the phone rang, Jason jumped a mile. He spoke briefly to Brandy and hung up. "Mr. Gammel?" Jason couldn't look at Gamma Rays. He couldn't look at Eddie either. It was hard enough looking at Tiny.

After a long moment, Jason picked up the remote. When Gamma Rays gave him the word, Jason pushed the button.

Zappo!

As easily as he came, Tiny was gone.

Chapter 20

Countdown

Return to sender, address unknown.
No such number, no such zone.

Eyes that had focused on the telephone now focused on the clock. Jason only hoped Gamma Rays's theories would work.

Too nervous to talk, Jason motioned to Eddie. They sat down on either side of Gamma Rays in front of the color monitor. The background shone bright blue with a random pattern of yellow *X*s.

"Eureka! There he is." Gamma Rays placed his finger on the blinking red cursor at the bottom right of the screen, representing Tiny. The *X*s represented stars.

12:02:05

Jason glanced anxiously at Eddie and was shocked. Eddie was the picture of fear, face drawn and tight, lips dry, shoulders hunched inward as he stared, transfixed, at the screen. I wonder if that's how I look, Jason thought, trying to swallow as his eyes returned to watch the blinking red cursor.

But where was it?

Jason leaned forward, not believing what he saw—a blue screen, yellow Xs, but no blinking cursor. Quickly he stood up to get a closer view.

"Hey, it's gone." Jason's voice cracked. "The cursor—Tiny. It's gone."

Gamma Rays hit the ENTER key. In an instant, another screen appeared with Xs in a different location. The cursor was back and blinking brightly.

"Hey, neat!" Eddie yelled. "Another galaxy."

Jason resumed breathing while his heartbeat returned to normal. For a minute he'd thought maybe Tiny had taken a wrong turn after the planet Pluto.

12:32:13

Jason sat on the edge of his seat. His eyes burned and his lip hurt from biting too hard. The cursor—Tiny—was moving up the screen now. More Xs appeared, some of them closer than before. It was beginning to resemble an obstacle course. Worried, Jason glanced at Gamma Rays. What if Tiny hit one?

Clearly, the same disaster had occurred to Gamma Rays. Suddenly the scientist hunched over the keyboard. His fingers flew as he pulled one program after the other, answering questions and calculating. Finally a six-digit number appeared across the bottom of the screen.

"Perfect!" Gamma Rays wiped the sweat off his wide forehead with the side of one arm. "Let's see how Tiny's doing relative to his mother." He brought up graphs in bright colors. "I wrote this program myself," Gamma Rays told them proudly. "It's a measurement of the magnetic bond I explained earlier. Notice how it grows in intensity as your little mastodon friend travels closer to his mother."

It was true. What was yellow, yellow-orange, and orange at the bottom, was bright pink and growing red, redder, redder.

Jason glanced at the clock.

12:57:10

Less than a minute to go!

Jason dried his slick palms on his jeans. This was awful. Even with his best friend and Gamma Rays beside him in the room, he'd never felt so alone.

Please don't ring, Jason told the phone, too afraid and superstitious to look at it. Let Tiny reach his mother first.

And then what Jason feared would happen

happened. The phone did ring. Still staring at the screen, Jason lifted the receiver from its cradle. Brandy did all the talking. The men had finished their lunch and were returning to the construction site.

Jason didn't need reminding. The slightest fluctuation in power could leave Tiny in a hundred million particles, all of them stranded between worlds. Or it could dump him in the worst possible situation in another zone. Anything from saber-tooth tigers to Cro-Magnon hunters to poison darts was possible. How could he have taken such risks with his pet?

Jason wiped his nose with the back of his hand. He rubbed his eyes dry with his shoulder. A high-pitched beeping brought Jason back to attention.

Suddenly the screen flashed scarlet.

"Wheee-oooo! Wheeeeeeeeeeeeeeeeeee-oooo!" Gamma Rays shouted. He banged enthusiastically on the desk as Eddie flew from his seat and began dancing around the room.

Too stunned to move, Jason felt Eddie's arms grab him by the shoulders. He heard Eddie holler in his ear as warm tears streamed down his cheeks.

Tiny was in the Pleistocene. Safe. With his mother.

Chapter 21

That's the Wonder

When Jason left Mr. Gammel's basement, he could have cartwheeled the whole way home. Everything Jason looked at glowed, even—and most of all—Brandy.

Jason was standing in the living room, staring anxiously out the window, when Brandy came barreling up the driveway. Her lips were pressed together in a tight line, her face flushed. Except for the blond hair and jogging shorts, Jason might have mistaken her for an angry locomotive.

With a loud whoosh Brandy pushed open the front door and headed for the stairs. Jason expected her to pester him about his science experiment. She didn't.

Jason heard the louder than usual sprongy sound of bedsprings. When the stereo snapped on, Jason tiptoed up the steps.

"That other girl was there too," he heard Brandy say angrily into the phone. "Honestly, what do you *expect* I would do? I told him in no uncertain terms if he landed his buns in a basket of french fries, I could care less. That cheating, lying, faithless skunk."

Brandy hung up the phone and made another call. Each time, when Brandy didn't say *why* she was at McDonald's in the first place, Jason was ecstatic.

Nobody had a sister as magnificent as Brandy Richards.

In a daze, Jason slipped quietly down the stairs. He walked out the back door, past the tent still standing from the night before, and into the woods, where he and Eddie had agreed to meet in order to clean up the clearing. There, Jason stopped dead in his tracks, completely unprepared for what he saw.

The clearing was empty.

Oh, there was a log and a trash can half-filled with water. There were two rumpled sleeping bags, neither of which seemed connected to Jason in any way. Cereal bowls lay on the grass, a dead fly floating in one; a rake, a pitchfork, scattered piles of grass clippings, a Frisbee, and a Nerfball.

But there was no Tiny.

There was no red furry little fellow, eyes sparkling, trunk extended in a happy greeting, tail twitching with excitement. There was no squeal, no thud, thud, thud. No munching or scrunching. There was nothing for the sun's rays to catch and turn to spun copper.

There was only a dull ache inside of Jason and a clearing bigger and greener and emptier than when he had left it.

Jason collapsed on the log. He bent his head until it met the folded arms resting on his knees, and he cried. How special was this clearing in the woods without Tiny? What good was this log? Why should the sun bother to shine if its fingers couldn't spin Tiny's coat to copper?

Sniffling, Jason raised his head. His foot knocked against something on the ground. The rubber brush he'd used only yesterday on Tiny! Jason picked it up and threw it as hard as he could. Then he put his head down and cried some more.

For the first time in his life, Jason knew the word *heartbreak.* His chest hurt with such intensity, he wondered how he'd manage to breathe the rest of the day. And even that didn't really matter.

A twig snapped behind him.

"Tiny?" Jason whirled.

"Just me."

With two steps, Eddie sat down on the log beside Jason. For the longest time, neither boy said a word as they built a wall of emptiness between them and then, stone by stone, slowly tore it down.

"I'm never coming back here again. Don't you try to make me either," Jason said angrily.

Jason could barely stop himself from slamming into Eddie. He wanted—needed—badly to hit something, anything, *anybody*, as if hurting someone else would diminish the hurt inside of him. It was no different than Brandy mouthing off to Dad.

Jason sobbed bitterly and without shame. "What kind of world is this if I can't have my baby mastodon?"

Eddie got up from the log. He took a swipe at a branch and, keeping his back turned to Jason, wiped his nose on his sleeve. This time, Jason knew it wasn't an allergy.

"You miss him too?" Jason sniffled.

"What do you think?" Eddie yelled so loud birds flew from the trees. "You think I'm stupid? Of course, I miss him. I might have complained, but I still liked him." He stopped to clear his throat. "For whatever it's worth, Jase, you did the right thing."

"Yeah. Then how come it feels so lousy?"

"I don't know, but it stinks and I don't mean the poop." When Eddie tried to laugh at his own joke, it came out in hiccups. He took another hard swing and knocked the trash barrel over until all the water ran out. Then he gave it a kick, sending the barrel crashing into the bushes. "Gosh, what if we'd had him more than a week? I bet you never thought of that. Think how awful that would be. I mean, if we miss him now, think how much we'd miss him after a year or two." Eddie picked up the barrel. Looking awkward as a puppy, he carried it over to where Jason was sitting. "So, now what do we do?"

"There's nothing to do. I keep expecting him to come up behind one of those bushes. I keep thinking I see him out of the corner of my eye." Jason sighed so deeply his whole body shook. "I guess we clean this place up like we planned."

"Leave it like it was. I'll get the sleeping bags."

"And then," Jason said, wiping his eyes with the bottom of his T-shirt, "we ought to go back to see Gamma Rays."

"What?" Eddie shrieked. "Didn't you have enough?"

"No. We owe Gamma Rays. You know how grown-ups have to sign a bunch of covenants when they move into our neighborhood? The covenants say what you can and can't do. We ought to read them in case there's a loophole." Jason waited for Eddie to say something. When he didn't, Jason added, "I know about loopholes because of what my mother does at her office."

"Uh-oh," Eddie sang, rolling his eyes as he did. "You're going to get us in trouble." He shrugged. "What the heck. Let's go."

Gamma Rays had the covenants in a strongbox with his other important papers.

"Hey, look!" Jason said after a few minutes of reading. "It says you can't park a boat in your driveway or on your curb. It says you can't put anything out of the ordinary in your yard or construct a fence or shed without approval. It doesn't say anything about what you can put on your roof."

"What about Santa Claus?" Eddie joked.

Jason frowned. "It doesn't say. It doesn't say you can't put a satellite dish on your roof either."

Stunned, Gamma Rays took the document from Jason and read it for himself. "Why, you're absolutely one hundred percent correct. Jason, you found the loophole." He tapped the list of covenants with the back of his hand. "There is nothing in here about a roof."

"So, would your satellite dish work up there?" Jason asked.

Gamma Rays rubbed his chin thoughtfully. "Actually, we might get even better reception. We'd have to bolt the dish to the chimney and run wires down the side of the house. A piece of cake!"

"Great! We'll help!" Jason and Eddie laughed.

"Don't forget what I promised my sister," Jason added. "We have to tilt the satellite dish toward Memphis."

Gamma Rays was right. Working together, what they had to do wasn't difficult.

Two hours later, Jason and Eddie entered the Richards's kitchen.

"Jason! I'm waiting!"

"You have the remote?" Eddie asked.

"Yeah." Jason tapped his pocket lightly with his finger as they headed toward the living room.

Brandy was sitting on the couch, legs folded. On the opposite side of the room, leaning against the chair, was a giant poster of Elvis Presley.

She had two cans of soda on the coffee table. Also a big bowl of pretzels.

Jason plopped down on the couch beside her. Eddie took the other side.

"Here," Jason said, handing Brandy the remote. "Just do what I told you."

Brandy glanced from Jason to Eddie. "This better not be some joke," she said. "I don't want to look stupid. You guys can't tell."

"We're not going to tell. That's part of the deal," Jason reminded her. "You can't tell either."

"OK." Brandy pointed the remote at the poster, her eyes intent. Concentrating, she pressed the button.

"*Zap. Zap. Zappo.* C'mon, Elvis. *Zappo. Zappo.*"

Jason and Eddie glanced at each other and shrugged.

Suddenly—*Twang! Twang!*—a loud guitar almost blew them out of their seats. Half a second later, the room filled with the sound, energy, and presence of a familiar baritone, followed by Brandy's squeal of shock and total frenzy.

When no one else can understand me,
When everything I do is wrong,
You give me love and consolation
You give me hope to carry on.

You're always there to lend a hand
In all I try to do . . .

Just then the phone rang. Jason reached back for the cordless, covering his ear so he could hear who was on the other end.

Jason tapped Brandy's arm. He raised his eyebrows and pointed to the telephone, indicating it was for her. Brandy shook her head.

"Sorry," Jason said into the receiver. "She's got somebody else she's more interested in."

Jason put the phone back on the coffee table. Then he leaned back on the couch, propped his feet up, and enjoyed the show.

Guess I'll never know the reason why
You love me as you do.
That's the wonder,
The wonder of you.